The Bookweaver's Daughter

by
Malavika Kannan

Tanglewood • Indianapolis

Published by Tanglewood Publishing, Inc.
© 2020 Malavika Kannan

Cover Design by Karina Granda
Interior Design by Amy Alick Perich

Tanglewood Publishing, Inc.
1060 N. Capitol Ave., Ste. E-395
Indianapolis, IN 46204
www.tanglewoodbooks.com

Printed by Sheridan in the U.S.A.
10 9 8 7 6 5 4 3 2 1

ISBN: 978-1-939100-41-2

Library of Congress Control Number: 2020934905

DEDICATION

This book is for everyone who felt like their
favorite books weren't woven for them.

For all the girls who looked for a
heroine in their bathroom mirrors.

For a twelve-year-old writer who thought
she wasn't magical. This one's for you.

CONTENTS

If the radiance of a thousand suns burst at once into the sky,

That would be like the splendor of the Mighty One.

I would become Death, the Shatterer of Worlds.

The Bhagavad Gita

Prologue

The problem with weaving stories is that you can never quite know when yours will begin.

I didn't.

What I did know was that the magic had always been a part of me, potent as burning stars and night-colored dreams. And so was danger, following the magic like a filly following a mare. In a kingdom where legacies were at war, these were the only two things I was certain of.

But I'm getting ahead of myself.

The Bookweaver named me after the *reya* flowers that bloom in Kasmira every spring: luminous and silver, like shards of broken pearl. "Reya Kandhari," he once told me. "A powerful name for a powerful girl."

I sometimes think it's the sight of rippling silver *reya* fields that first inspired me to write. I wanted to capture all of that beauty and enigma and save it from the darkness.

My father once dreamed of placing the traditional wreath of *reya* on my brow and passing his gift down to me. But that dream had been ripped apart years ago, tearing with it a girl with a legacy for a last name, and leaving an unfinished tale in her place.

Then all I had were the words and the pressing, bone-deep cold.

One

The Bookweaver once told me that when we die, we all leave something behind.

A cobbler leaves behind a legacy of warmly clad feet; a baker leaves behind memories of sated stomachs; a writer leaves behind a testament to our humanity. You can leave behind a book or a house or a child. Really, it can be anything, as long as it was once warm from your touch and alight with your fire and carries a piece of you within it forever.

The problem is, he said, we don't realize the gravity of our duty until we're forced to act. We find ourselves unanchored, and that's when we realize that we forgot to leave our mark. And by then, there's no turning back.

"*Reya Patel.*"

The sound of the name that I used in the Fields jarred me back to reality. I looked down from my tree branch to see Lord Gilani, the overlord, glaring at me.

"Are you expecting the mangoes to harvest themselves, Patel?"

I took a deep breath.

"No," I said. "I'm almost done."

Gilani rolled his eyes. "I need another half-bushel before sundown. Get to work."

I envisioned the mango tree toppling down on him as I slung my basket over my shoulder and started to climb.

A strong branch, laden with mangoes, loomed over my head, and I wrestled its fruit into the basket with vengeance. And then I continued to climb, because in moments like this, it felt easier to leave my anger on the ground.

From the treetop, I could see the Fields unfolded before me: the orchards, the pastures, and other peasants toiling in the heat. Beyond that sprawled the entire *Raj*— raucous bazaars, clay gardens, and homes painted brightly to ward off demons. Pearl-tipped minarets that challenged the heavens themselves. And most hauntingly, the royal *mahal,* reflected a thousand times in rivers unspooling like silk.

Once the basket was full, I tied it to a pulley and lowered it to the ground. As the basket descended, I remembered what my father once told me about the cosmic laws of *karma*. I wondered what I'd done to get mine so out of balance, and how long I had to wait until the universe repaid its debt.

Down below, a gray-eyed girl hefted the basket onto her shoulder and squinted up at me.

"Reya?" she called.

Nina's voice was steady enough, but her eyes kept darting up to the sky, where storm clouds were gathering. A cold wind washed over the Fields, sending crops rippling. The storm was going to be especially bad today—I could see it in the restless pacing of the over-lords, the hushed whispers, and the billowing darkness descending upon us.

Somehow—and perhaps I was imagining it, but I picked up on the stench of decay, laced within the drowsy scent of mangoes—I couldn't shake the feeling that something was stirring. A story waiting to unfold, a legend in the making.

"You look depressed," Nina continued matter-of-factly. "You promised me that the angsty phase was over."

She smiled at me. For a moment, it felt like we were still eight years old, and it was my first day of mandatory service in the Fields. I had just scraped my knee on a branch, and she had reached for me with that same smile. I knew right then when she took my hand, she was also taking a piece of my heart. In spite of the secrets I kept from her, there was something about Nina Nadeer that made me certain that scraped knees could be healed, rain storms could be weath-ered, and humans could leave their mark.

"You worry too much about me," I called down, resisting the urge to check the sky again. "I'll be fine."

Her eyes crinkled a little, like she didn't quite believe me.

"I've been meaning to tell you," she said. "There's a rumor that there's going to be a raid on the Fringes soon, so be careful going home tonight. King Jahan's on a witch hunt for rebels."

I ignored the twist in my stomach.

"Forcing us all to work the Fields isn't enough for

him?" I said. "The Zakirs drove out the Mages seven
years ago. There's literally nobody left to rebel."

"They're getting paranoid," said Nina sagely, stoop-
ing back over the mangoes. "I don't blame them. These
are dangerous times."

I opened my mouth to respond, and that's when I
felt it.

Heat seared the skin between my collarbones, so
fleeting but powerful that I nearly fell off the branch. I
rolled completely sideways, one hand clutching the
fork of the tree, the other reaching for the pearl I wore
on my neck.

Someone screamed as the branch tipped precariously, sliding out of my grip. I flailed, fingers scrabbling on the decaying bark—it was smooth, entirely
too smooth—and even as the blood rushed into my
head, all I could hear was the screaming. I wished it
would stop.

Right before the branch broke, I realized the
screams were mine.

There was an awful crack, and for a moment, I was
suspended in midair—nothing but iron-colored clouds,
a clean blank page—then the ground rushed at me as
I tumbled, broken branch and all, landing flat on my
back.

"Ni—Nina—" I couldn't get the words out.

"Reya!" Nina dropped her basket and pulled me to
my feet. Vaguely, I heard her fuss over me, but I
couldn't focus on that—only the panic, clawing its way
up my throat.

My pearl was an illegal amulet, and its lifeblood
was connected to my father's. If it was discovered, I
could be accused of being a Mage. I'd never under-

stood how the pearl worked, but its meaning was devastating: if it burned, my father's life was in danger. If I was too late, it would shatter.

I hadn't imagined it: the pearl had burned. And that could only mean one thing. The Bookweaver was in danger.

I could feel the pearl throbbing against my heartbeat. I had to get home to him.

Thunder rumbled through the clouds, and the skies split at last, releasing a horrible fury on the peasants below. I stumbled forward, and Nina stretched out her hand.

The thunder sounded like a thousand pearls spilled by a careless hand, the beating *tabla* drums for a riot of rain and wind. I could barely see where I was going: only Nina's hand guided me through the stampede of people. Despite her comforting presence, my panic was rising.

I slipped my hand out of Nina's, but she held on tight. "Don't lose me," she shouted over the wind. "I know where we can find shelter—"

"Let go," I said, tugging against her grip. She whirled around, confused. "But you'll get trampled—"

"Be careful," I managed, and then I wrenched my hand free from Nina's. She reached for me, frantic, but the chaos swept her away, her shouts drowned beneath an army of thundering feet.

I'm sorry, I wanted to shout. But I didn't. She wouldn't have heard me, anyways.

I cut through the orchards, pulling my hood up as I ran. Herding as one against the staggering winds, nobody noticed a lone girl escaping into the forbidden outskirts of the Fields.

There it stood: the Fields' wall. It kept hungry animals out—and hungry peasants in. Almost anyone would assume the wall was impassable. But I'm not one of those people, and neither was my mother. When I was younger, she used to remind me, *"There's always a way out if you're persistent enough to find it."* She was right. After weeks of scoping, I had found the vulnerability: a single loose stone. It took a few blows from a shovel before the stone gave way. For seven years, it had remained my only means of escape.

I gave a sharp push, and the stone slid out, revealing a narrow opening. Through the gap, I caught a glimpse of the rain-soaked streets of the *Raj*.

Before slipping through the gap, I looked back at the Fields: at the flat blankets of red-packed earth, the bowed orchards of mango trees, and—maybe I was just imagining it—Nina's forlorn gray eyes. And then I was gone.

Kasmira's crooked streets, normally teeming with peddlers, cowherds, and wandering minstrels, were abandoned. The colorful *rangoli* that usually adorned doorsteps had been washed away, leaving blood-colored stains on the footpaths. Only the royal *mahal*, dark and foreboding in the distance, stood firm beyond the lashing rain.

I caught a glimpse of myself in a darkened window as I ran, and my expression startled me. Beneath the hood of my cloak, my green eyes were unrecognizable. They didn't look scared. They looked wild.

The sky was filmy and dark by the time I reached our home—a crumbling cottage at the edge of the Fringes. Even after seven years, our shop carried scars of battle: burn marks on the walls, sword gouges in the clay-baked streets. To some of Kasmira's most oppressed, these marks represented resistance from the time Jahan Zakir first took over.

To me, they served as a warning: we could hide, but we could never truly escape the king.

I knocked on our door, proclaimed by a hand-painted sign to be a bookbinder's workshop.

"Father?"

There was no answer.

I pounded again. "It's me. You can open up."

Silence.

My stomach turned, and in spite of myself, my fingers were trembling as I fumbled for my key. "I'm coming in—"

I swung open the door, and the firelight engulfed me.

My father was curled in the corner, hidden behind mountains of green hide and vellum. Wax lamps dripped freely onto his desk, but he didn't seem to notice. He was writing with an almost religious fervor, oblivious to the rest of the world—including his daughter at the door.

Relief made my hands shake, and I slipped them into my pockets to hide their tremor.

"I'm home," I said at last, because I didn't know what else to say.

My father looked up and noticed me at last. He beckoned me inside. "Reya," he murmured. "You're early."

He caught sight of my expression and frowned. "Your hands are shaking in your pockets."

I forced a smile. "You weren't feeling well today, and Nina warned me about a raid in the Fringes," I said. "I guess I got scared."

"The pearl didn't burn, did it?" he said, looking concerned.

There was something about the way he spoke that gave it away, every time. Because although he was disguised as a lowly bookbinder, Amar Kandhari was the Bookweaver, Kasmira's patron of literature. He was one of the three Yogis, the ancient guardians of Kasmira. He was also my father.

"No," I lied. "Nothing like that. But it's good to see you writing again." I touched his feet briefly before rising to check his temperature.

"Your forehead is scalding. Why didn't you take anything for it?"

The Bookweaver smiled weakly, but his eyes didn't quite meet mine. "It's just a fever," he said. "I've been burning up all day. But it's nothing for you to worry about."

I exhaled slowly. He was getting weaker every season. I rarely allowed myself to think about it, but I was always afraid he wouldn't pull through.

"Did you drink the *rasam*?" I asked, crouching beside the fire for warmth.

My father frowned, and I realized that the *rasam* I'd made for him this morning lay untouched in its pot. "Honestly, Reya, I haven't felt hungry for hours."

I bit my lip. If he couldn't even bring himself to eat, then the illness was worse than I'd feared.

"It doesn't matter," I said, sounding much more confident than I felt. "You've got to keep up your strength. That's the only way you can fight this thing."

He watched me silently as I heated the *rasam* in the pot. His expression was unreadable—I wondered if he suspected things were far worse than I was letting on.

The aroma of warm spices began to permeate the shop. I was grateful for the cheerily bubbling pot and roaring rain for filling the guilty silence between us.

"I promise it'll taste better hot," I said, passing him a steaming bowl. "It's not as good as Mom's, but still—"

His reproachful eyes met mine, and I stopped mid-sentence.

I had forgotten how fragile he could be on days like this. Huddled behind his bookbinding supplies, it wasn't hard to pretend that the Bookweaver was a child himself. Only his expression, deep-set and grieving, belied his actual age.

The roof creaked in protest against the drumming rain, drowning out the hissing pot and my father's labored breaths. The *rasam* seemed to be working: he set the bowl aside and looked me in the face for the first time that day.

"Reya," he started, and the pain in his voice was palpable, like bruises beneath skin. "I'm sorry."

I bit back the old rage I thought I had conquered. It was awful to resent my father, broken as he was from Jahan's crusade. But somehow, it felt like *I* was more of the parent. It felt like I protected him from the world, not the other way around. I knew what was at stake—I knew the power of the legacy we were safeguarding—but that didn't always make things easier. Not on days like this.

"I don't want to hear it," I said, enclosing his hand in mine. "No apologies until you're better."

He still looked stricken, so I shifted closer to him and leaned against his shoulder. It was bony and frail beneath my weight, but I knew he was grateful for the gesture.

"What are you writing about today?" I asked, glancing at his manuscript. Beneath the dense forest of script was an illumination of three wizened Mages. Ever since the monsoons started, my father had been writing down our forbidden myths and folktales—*our heritage,* he called it. I could almost sense the paper breathing, whispering its tales to me if I stopped to listen.

"The legend of the first *Yogis,*" he said. "I finally got around to writing it down. You used to love that story."

He still wasn't looking at me, but I recognized the peace offering. It was his promise that things could be better between us.

"I never stopped loving your stories," I said softly.

He smiled. "You're a Kandhari," he said. "It's in your blood."

I flipped through the pages, careful not to smear the ink. Within them, I could sense the power of the tapestries handed down by our ancestors—vengeful gods who lived on mountain peaks. Grotesque and gentle monkey-beasts. Demons who ruled kingdoms cloaked by darkness. The elegance of his books reminded me of the Bookweaver himself: a shadow of goodness that didn't quite belong in this dark, harsh place.

"Tens of thousands of years ago," I began quietly. Father closed his eyes to listen, his face serene. I tilted the book towards the lamplight and began to read aloud.

Tens of thousands of years ago, they say Kasmira was a barren desert—as magnificent and lonely as an ancient tome. There were no hissing cobras, flying elephants, or jungles glittering like jewels. It was a blank slate, a silent promise. It was waiting for a miracle.

And so the gods poured forth great pools of water, fire, and earth—and then, they built a woman. This first woman was wiser than an elephant. She took the elements, scattered them around the desert, and from there, a kingdom was born. She filled Kasmira with animals, and finally, humans: small, blind creatures struggling towards self-preservation. But the woman was not finished, for she knew that there was something beyond survival: there was life.

And so she gave birth to three great children who would become the legendary Yogis. The first heir, the Lightweaver, could craft anything with his fair fingers. Next was the Songweaver, who filled valleys with her lovely music. Last came the Bookweaver, who raised cities with his words and ideas. Together, the three Yogis were the very spirit of humanity.

But then the curse of mankind—greed and jealousy—crept into their powerful hearts. They overthrew their mother and fought each other for dominance. They would have killed each other if not for the Bookweaver's counsel, which saved them from doom. The Yogis realized that alone, they were only one aspect, but together, they were the heart of humanity. At last, they decided that they would pass their powers down to their children so their legacies could create inspiration throughout Kasmira.

I turned the page, but the other side was empty. Disappointment spidered through me. "What happens next?"

Father opened his eyes, and it was as though a spell had been broken. He no longer looked serene. In the dying firelight, he looked exhausted.

"You know the rest," he said. "Our ancestors picked up the tradition. Then I did. Then you will. The story isn't finished. It won't finish. Not any time soon, at least."

I wanted to ask him what he meant, but just then, the sun split the clouds, suffusing the workshop in light. The storm was clearing, which meant that I had mere minutes before Lord Gilani started looking for me.

"I have to get back to the Fields," I said. "Father, promise me you're going to finish the story before I'm home again."

He smiled. He said something to me, he must have.

To this day, try as I might, I can never remember exactly what my father said to me as I headed out of the cottage. I remember feeling the warmth of his gaze even after I closed the door, but I cannot remember his last words.

It was only when I was at least a mile from the crumbling Fringes that I finally tucked my pearl back beneath my shirt and allowed myself to breathe.

"Halt!"

I jerked back instinctively, catching a glimpse of a blue-turbaned uniform. Standing at the edge of the lane was an imperial soldier. Our eyes met.

For a second, all I could see was the sword at his belt. Then I leapt into action and darted down the street, disappearing around a corner before he could get a good look at me.

My strides were starting to slow, but new footsteps began thundering behind me. To my horror, three more soldiers were gaining on me.

"Girl!" one of them shouted. "What are you doing? Shouldn't you be at home with your mother?" He surveyed my ragged clothes and wild eyes. "Or up to no good, are you?"

He lunged without warning, and I skittered away just in time, adrenaline shooting up my veins. "Chase her!"

I heard his comrades shouting behind me, and I tore through the bazaar, my breath sawing in my lungs. The streets of the *Raj* blurred like whirled-up water as I ran.

My legs, which burned at first, were completely numb by the time I reached the wall of the Fields. The stone fell aside at my tug, and I dove through the narrow gap. My fingers made brief contact with the grass on the other side before someone grabbed my ankle.

I could never remember what my father said to me, but I can't forget this: I didn't tell my father I loved him.

Two

My fingers scratched the wall for traction, blood singing in my ears. The hand on my ankle felt like a vise—I couldn't shake it off—

In that moment, I did the natural thing. The man pulled me up, and before either of us had fully realized what I was doing, I bit him until I tasted blood.

"*Aargh!*"

The man swore and jerked away; I seized my chance to fling myself from his grasp. My knees took the impact as I landed hard on the ground and rolled to my feet—

A second hand shot out of nowhere. There was only enough time to scream before someone shoved me against the wall.

"It's just a kid!" he shouted in surprise.

"Well, she sure doesn't bite like one," said another voice gruffly.

My captor turned me around so he could see my

face. I felt my stomach sink. The man before me was wearing the official imperial uniform of the *Raj*, and the captain's turban was embellished with a bronze *Z*.

They worked for the Zakir dynasty.

"What do you think you're doing, peasant?" the captain snarled.

For a moment, all I could do was stare at the bronze *Z*, unable to form words. In the bright sun, it glinted like a lightning bolt hurled down by vengeful gods.

The captain glared at me. Teeth marks oozed on his hand, and in spite of everything, I felt a surge of savage pleasure. "This is excellent," he said angrily. "Her mouth worked well enough when she was biting me."

He rubbed his hand indignantly as voices called from down the street. "Hold her, officers!"

The imperial soldiers who had been chasing me finally turn the corner, panting. "What's your name, girl?" the first one demanded.

"Reya Patel," I choked out, which was the name I used in the Fields. As the imperial soldiers conferred, I could still taste the captain's blood in my mouth, hollow and tinny.

"Very well, Miss Patel," the soldier said at last, his voice dangerously calm. "What were you doing in a rough neighborhood like the Fringes? Won't your mother be looking for you?"

"My mother's dead," I answered truthfully, and his eyebrows rose.

"How about … your father?" he asked. There was something in his voice that made my breath catch in my throat. *My father.*

He knew.

I licked my lips, but they didn't moisten.

"No, sir," I said. "I work in the Fields. When the storm broke, I was trying to find shelter, and I ended up on the streets, and I was just coming back when your soldiers chased me and I panicked, and ..."

I trailed off lamely, realizing how bad my lie was only after it was out of my mouth.

The captain I had bitten spoke up. "Let's just haul her to Prince Devendra. It's not like anyone's going to miss her—she's got no mother."

The soldier who had been interrogating me shook his head. He was still peering into my eyes, as if looking for signs of untrustworthiness.

"There's no need to waste the prince's time over a silly child," he said. "I say we bring her back to the Fields and let Lord Gilani deal with the punishment."

The captain nodded curtly. "All right, Miss Patel," he said. "We'll be keeping a *very* close watch on you. Another step out of line, and we won't be quite so lenient." He saluted the other soldiers and started to march me away.

I dared to glance back at the imperial soldier who had just interrogated me. I saw his brooding eyes zero in on mine. He didn't know my real name, didn't know where I lived, but I still had an eerie feeling he knew exactly who I was.

Then the soldier turned on his heel and walked out of sight.

"Don't give me any trouble," the captain growled, "when we get there. You stand to be fined or even fired for desertion."

I took a deep breath, almost shivering with relief. I was alive, and so was my father, even if it was only for another minute.

A couple peasants were lounging by the gate to the Fields, chewing *neem* leaves and playing mancala. They snapped to attention at the sight of the captain. "Call for Lord Gilani," he said gruffly. "We have a stray worker."

The gates creaked open, and Gilani appeared. The captain filled him in, and Gilani's brows contracted. "Rest assured that Miss Patel will be punished."

I took a deep breath, my back already aching from all the mangoes I'd harvest after I took a sound scolding. The captain released his grip on my arm and marched off, still clutching his bite wound. Lord Gilani waited until he was out of sight before he dragged me through the Fields.

"These aren't the days of the Mages anymore, Miss Patel," he snarled. "This is the reign of Jahan Zakir. We don't put up with peasant filth. Do you know what happens to rebellious little girls under the new order?"

Fury unfurled in my chest. I focused on my heartbeat, hot and incandescent, as he marched me back to the mango groves. Peasants stopped to stretch their backs and stare as Gilani strode past.

"Of course," I said, in a tight little voice that did not belong to me. I had just caught sight of a tall, dark-haired girl rushing past the cow sheds. Without waiting for Lord Gilani to dismiss me, I started after Nina.

She was shoving through a barley field, leaving a trampled path of bronze stalks in her wake. Although I was running, my stride was half of hers. By the time I caught up to her, I was panting.

"Wait!"

She turned around, and something in her expression made me pause. Her eyes contained a sadness I had never seen in them before.

"Nina?" I asked warily.

Her face fell. "Sometimes I feel like I don't know you," she said, pointing an accusing finger at me. "What were you thinking, disappearing on me and nearly getting arrested?"

My stomach dropped, as if it was not a finger, but a sword that she was pointing at me.

"Nina, try to understand," I started, though I certainly didn't. "I know I've been hiding things from you. Just hear me through—"

But clearly, she wasn't going to.

"Seven years, and I never asked questions," she said. Her voice was cold, as though we were already strangers. "I knew there were some things you didn't want to tell me. But if you're running into trouble with imperial soldiers, don't you think I should have known?"

"Nina—"

She cut across sharply. "Your secrecy will be the death of us," she said. "I try so hard to protect you—"

That stung. Now it was my turn to get angry.

"You're not the only person in the Fields dealing with all sorts of darkness, did you consider that?" I said. "Maybe I'm up against a lot more than you think. Maybe I'm trying to protect you. How would you know?"

"That's right, how *would* I know? You never told me!"

There was a pause in which we simply stared at each other.

"You know what?" Nina said suddenly. "Nobody gives a damn about what happens to girls like us, Reya. I thought we were supposed to stick together.

But you're out for yourself, just like everyone else in this cursed kingdom."

I was startled to see tears clinging to her lashes. She wiped her eyes, but they flowed freely, as though she'd been holding them down for years and they'd finally gotten the best of her.

"What I really want is stability," she said, no longer looking at me. "I want someone who'd be there for me, who'd live their truth, who'd *choose* me until the end of the world. But clearly, you'd just as soon leave—"

"Nina, that's not true, and we both know it!" I said, before I could stop myself. "If I could tell you the truth, I would. You have to believe me."

"I would trust you with my life. I thought you felt the same," she said. "Where did you go today?"

I took a deep breath. "Home," I said. "I thought my father was in danger. With all the raids, I thought—"

"But your father's a bookbinder, not a rebel." Nina frowned. "Right?"

I bit my lip. "Nina—"

Her eyes darkened. Nina had every reason to hate me; I'd just let her down irreparably. The door of lies between my world and hers had opened just a crack, and all sorts of hell was coming loose. There was no way to fix that.

Actually, there was. I could tell her the truth.

But in doing so, I would be terribly endangering the Bookweaver. Was I truly going to put my best friend before my father?

My head screamed *No*, but a little part of me, the part of me that was selfish and resentful towards my father, was screaming louder.

I looked into Nina's eyes, the precise color of the clearing storm clouds above. It really wasn't a choice.

"I want you to join me at sunset," I said. "There's something I think you should know."

The sun finally set, staining the sky with shadowed ink. Nina and I hung up our baskets and headed out the gate. I was fully aware of everyone staring at me as I passed. Slowly, the bone-weary peasants rumbled out of the Fields in masses, a defeated army stumbling towards retreat.

Nina still wasn't speaking to me. She'd said nothing as we walked through the darkening city, but when we turned into the Fringes, her curiosity got the best of her.

"Reya, wait," she said at last. "What are you trying to do?"

"I'm trying to tell you the truth," I said. "But once I do, there's no going back. It's going to be difficult. You could end up in danger."

She glanced at me briefly. "Try me," she said. And so I started with a simple, bald sentence.

"My father is the Bookweaver."

What did I expect, sudden recognition? Instead, her anger gave way to blank disbelief. "There's no way. He's a myth. He died seven years ago."

I met her eyes, holding her gaze steady with mine. "The myths are all true," I told her. "It started the day Jahan took over, when he drove the Mages out of Kasmira to secure the throne."

Nina's expression soured at the mention of the king. "I'm listening," she muttered.

"The truth is, I'm not actually a peasant," I said. "I'm the Bookweaver's daughter. The king tried to kill my father when I was eight years old."

I plunged on. "Magic was outlawed, forcing all the Mages and Yogis to flee. We chose to hide in plain sight, disguised as peasants. That's how I ended up in the Fields. It was the only way to protect my father's secret."

Nina hesitated. "But I've known you for seven years," she said. "I remember when you were drafted into the Fields. You've always been a peasant, just like me."

There was a touch of desperation in her voice, as if she was begging for confirmation that our entire friendship wasn't based on a lie.

I steeled my nerves, took a deep breath. "No, I'm not," I said quietly. "And my last name isn't Patel. It's Kandhari."

I saw her eyes light up in recognition. Her lips silently formed the fabled last name.

She was still frowning at me, but with less fury in her eyes. I could tell what she was thinking: my story made sense. She just had to decide whether it was true.

"No," she said at last. "Your name is Reya Patel. You're a bookbinder's daughter. I know you. *I know you.*"

Desperation had returned to her voice. I didn't blame her. The world was shattering under my feet, and I was pulling her down with me.

"You do," I insisted. "You do know me. Just not this side of me. Not that it changes anything—"

Nina looked like I'd slapped her.

"Of course this changes everything. You were near-ly arrested, and now you're telling me that your father is actually a lost Mage who everyone thought was dead—"

"Nina," I interrupted. "Do you believe me?"

She hesitated. "Of course I do, but—" She squinted at something behind me. "Reya, what is that?"

I whirled around to see something black and shapeless flowing across the street, thick and inscrutable as the marrow in my bones. Even from thirty feet away, even in the darkness, I picked up on its unmistakable scent.

"Smoke," I said. "Nina—"

And then my pearl started to burn.

Without waiting for a response, I tore down the street. Nina gasped, struggling to keep up with me. "What are you doing?"

Her eyes were wide and wild, her face reflecting my panic a thousand times over.

"My father. He's in danger," I choked out. "Something's happened. We need to find him. Hurry—" I pulled at her wrist. "*Hurry*—"

I turned the corner, and the ashes hit me face-first, sending me reeling back.

Smoke was pouring down the street, thick and scented with decay. It attacked us with vengeance: clawing our eyes, our throats, anywhere it found vulnerability. Coughing, Nina tugged me forward—and then, as the smoke parted, I saw it.

It was my father's home—the cottage that had stood firm against war and death and everything in between—except it was no longer our home. It had been razed to the ground. It was a burnt-out torch, a funeral pyre, an impossible magic trick—senseless, empty, *gone*.

And here's the thing.

You can live a whole life, filled with millions of moments that twist and blur like layers of chalk.

But no matter how many layers, minutes, seconds, years you put before it, there will be the Moment after which all bets are off. You can divide your entire existence neatly into pre-Moment and post-Moment. Because that Moment will never really leave you.

My throat closed as I reached for the pearl. My fingers struggled for a moment, then found it. The pearl was shattered, confirming what I knew deep down but simply could not accept: that this was my Moment, that the Bookweaver was dead.

I lurched towards the wreckage, only to feel Nina's grip tighten on my wrist. "Reya—" She was pleading with me, pulling me towards safety, but I wrenched myself free.

"Don't just stand there!" I snarled. "Do something! Dig! It's not too late. It's not too late. We can save him. It's not too late—"

The light in Nina's eyes was more than a reflection of the embers before us—it was its own conflagration, the kind of fire that melted my fury and brought my resolve crashing down.

"Nina, come on, please don't be stupid, don't give up—he's somewhere in there, we need to get him out, we need to rescue him—"

"Reya," she said despairingly, and something in her voice finally broke through the haze of my panic.

I raised my hands in surrender, as though my hands could protect me, as though they could block out her words, but they couldn't—they couldn't—

Nina took my hands in hers, and when she next

spoke, her voice was soft. "*Reya.* There's nothing you can do. There's nobody left in that house. We're on our own."

Three

For a moment, all I could do was stare at her, thought-less, breathless, useless. "But—"

Her grip was gentle but firm. "Reya, you're in shock right now. You need to breathe. Come on, breathe with me. *Breathe.*"

In spite of everything, I obeyed. I inhaled a great draft of smoky air. I exhaled. I inhaled. I exhaled again. And then, as the ashes settled, I cried.

Ever since the Zakirs took over, I'd prepared for this moment. I'd lived in its shadow, challenged it, made my peace with it—but still, I cried. I think it's strange that we shed tears in grief, because my grief is a burning fire.

We burn our dead in Kasmira. In that dark and endless moment, I finally understood why.

"Reya," Nina was saying urgently. "How did this happen? Who did this to him?"

"I don't know," I said, but my stomach was sinking. Because I *did* know who had done this. There was only one man capable of it: Jahan Zakir. He had been hunting the Bookweaver for seven years. And now that my father was gone, I had finally become the new Bookweaver.

And his new target.

"It was Jahan," I managed. "The king got to him. There's nowhere safe anymore—" I staggered to my feet, sickened and disoriented. Out of habit, I rubbed my father's pearl for reassurance, but it was cracked.

Nina was panicking. "I believe you. I believe you," she said. "But we need to find someone. We need to tell someone what happened—"

I whirled on her. "Who are we going to tell, Nina? The king? *The king who killed him?* There's nothing to do. I need to leave, now."

"*What?*"

I took a deep breath, and when I spoke next, my voice sounded like it belonged to someone else: cold, emotionless, matter-of-fact. "Nina, listen very carefully," I said. "I am the Bookweaver's daughter, which means that now it's my turn to protect my father's legacy. I'm the new Bookweaver. You have to let me go."

After an agonizing silence, Nina spoke.

"If we have a kingdom to escape," she said quietly, "we have to leave right away."

In spite of everything, I stopped and stared at her.

"*We* don't have a kingdom to escape," I said. "I do. You're going to stay here in the *Raj*. In the city you're safe."

She frowned. "What are you talking about? You don't actually expect me to sit around, waiting for you to get killed—"

"Don't be ridiculous. Nobody knows you were here. You can't be hurt. There's no way I'm letting you risk all that to come with me."

She shook her head. "Reya, I can't let you leave alone. It's too dangerous—"

"Aren't you listening? That's *exactly* why you can't come," I interrupted. "If they catch me, they will kill me like they killed my father. But you—I'm giving you a chance to live your own life. *Why won't you take it?*"

Nina stared back at me, her lip curled with a stubbornness I knew too well. "This isn't your choice to make," she said. "You'd do the same for me."

I looked up to see a glowing moon: time was running out.

"Fine," I said tersely. "You can come. But we need to get going."

I felt guilt, as if I was sentencing her to a life on the run. I wanted to take back the words, but my tongue wouldn't move. Somehow, I felt like I couldn't bear my burden alone.

"All right," she said. "If there's anything we can salvage from the house, we need to find it. Come on—"

Together, we sifted through the wreckage. There wasn't much left: a few bronze *rupam* coins. A handful of half-scorched dresses. An old knife and waterskin. And buried beneath his desk, miraculously unscathed amidst the ashes, was my father's book of Kasmiri mythology.

I opened the book. The pages were a little singed, but the ink remained legible. I thumbed through until I found what I was looking for: the legend of the Yogis. The last story my father had woven for me. I turned to the last page, the one that had been empty—

Except it was no longer unfinished.

The End of the Story
And so it was that the Yogis began to spin their threads, threads that became ensnarled and tangled as the years went by, warping in their looms. Weaving. Waiting.

Reya, you are the final thread in the fabric that your ancestors have unspooled over eons, and now you must take up the loom. It is time for you to discover your place in the tapestry and find your own pattern to follow. And that will be the greatest challenge of all.

I regret that I cannot be here to steady your hand, as my forefathers did for me. But I take comfort in the belief that you will finally be able to weave your own legacy, define your own truth, and tell your own story. You'll meet life head-on, overcome it, and master whatever comes next. For me, that's enough.

It has to be.
Your Father, Amar

I traced his signature with my finger, familiar as my own breath, hoping I could somehow absorb his left-over warmth, or wisdom, or whatever remained. His living hands had once traced this paper, shaping his dying wish. He had left me no cliffhangers. No unfinished stories. No loose ends.

I slipped my father's book in my cloak and tucked the broken pearl back beneath my shirt. I could always use a piece of him with me.

"Nina," I said, as evenly as I could. "I think I'm ready."

She took my hand, and together we jogged down the ashy street. This time, I didn't look back when I ran, leaving all but the most persistent memories in my wake.

One of my clearest memories of the Bookweaver is from the day he almost lost me.

When I was six, he'd built me a swing, dangling invitingly from the veranda of our bungalow. I remember squealing when he helped me stand on the swing, clutching the rope as tightly as I could. "You're not made of fine china," he'd reassured me. "You won't break."

He pushed me high into the air, and for a moment, all I could see was the sky, sprawling around me, embracing me, swallowing me. I could see the royal *mahal*, the Endless Jungle and the Fields—unable to contain myself, I leaned forward and crowed, my cries mixing with my father's cheers behind me.

In that moment, I knew what it felt like to fly. I was still afraid, but not that I would fall. I was afraid that if I could, I would take off and never look back.

I had twisted towards my father, hoping he could anchor me to my home, and somehow, the swing left my feet. I crashed into the garden pond, the reflected sky claiming me once more.

I have since forgotten the exhilarating swoop of soaring like a bird. All I can remember is my father's tear-stained face as he bandaged my scrapes. His words are woven into my memory forever: "Reya, you almost broke. I almost broke you."

I reached for him through the haze of numbing

tinctures. "I can't break," I said drowsily. "I'm not made of fine china."

He laughed, despite the tears. "No, you're certainly not. You're my unsinkable, unbreakable little girl."

But he was wrong. Perhaps it was best he was dead, because I could not bear the thought of him seeing me now, terrified to face the life that he'd sacrificed everything to build for me.

I could see it now: the dark lane that led out of the Fringes. Nina and I had been careful to avoid the turbaned soldiers standing guard along the streets. Still, by the time the clay towers of the main city came into view, the sun was rising.

"This is going to be the hardest part," I warned her quietly. "We're going to have to make it across the heart of the city in broad daylight. If you want to back out, now's the time."

Nina merely smiled. "Not a chance," she said. "Now, are we leaving or not?"

I took her hand. "Here goes nothing," I muttered, and together, we plunged into the bustling crowd.

We made it to the corner of the street before I realized something was horribly wrong.

Enormous crowds of people were crammed into the main road, jostling to form a rowdy queue. I craned my neck to see what was happening, but I couldn't see over the head of an irate man in front of me. Instead, I caught sight of the unmistakable gleam of swords—*soldiers*.

Immediately, I shrank back. People closed in around us, protesting and shoving to see what was happening. Nina stared at me, her face rigid, but there was nowhere for us to go. We were trapped.

"They're inspecting every person who leaves this

street," Nina hissed. She didn't need to say anything else—we both knew exactly who they were looking for.

Someone started screaming. Thirty feet ahead of us in the line, the soldiers had seized a girl—about my age and size—with short hair the same color as mine. She was struggling and arguing. "I don't know what you're talking about! I'm not *her*, I swear!"

The nearest soldier grasped her by the chin and turned her towards his commander, who scrutinized her carefully. "Our description is of a fifteen-year-old girl with long brown hair," I heard him mutter to his comrade. "Let her go."

Horrified, I turned to Nina. The crowd was slowly shuffling us closer to the checkpoint. It was too late to turn back without arousing suspicion.

Nina's brow was furrowed, thinking fast. "Come here," she whispered. I obeyed, and she pulled the knife out.

"Wait, what are you—"

"Stay still, Reya."

Nina pulled back my hood and seized my braid. I heard the swish of the knife, felt a tug at my lower scalp, and turned just in time to see my braid fall to the ground, where it quickly disappeared under the onslaught of feet.

"What the—" I touched the back of my neck, now tickled by short, frayed hair ends. I was just feet from the nearest soldier now. There was no time to think: I simply closed my eyes.

An impatient hand pushed the back of my bare neck forward. I turned to see Nina stumbling along behind me, and the street was open before us. We surged ahead—and just like that, we were free.

We were halfway through the bazaar before either
of us could muster the courage to speak again.

Nina looked apologetically at me. "I'm really sorry
I had to cut your hair, Reya," she said.

I tugged at the ends of my hair. "Are you joking,
Nina? That was brilliant. You just saved my life."

She still looked worried. "We're not safe yet. It's
only a matter of time before they realize they missed
you, and then there will be soldiers everywhere."

Nina was right. The main gate was swarmed with
soldiers, so we doubled back to a side exit, relying on
the bustle of people through the Raj to disguise us.

The side alleys were almost silent. Nina kept jumping at small noises, from the crunch of late summer
leaves to the slosh of water in sewage pipes. I reached
out and took her hand. I could feel her pulse racing
and knew that mine was, too.

"It's less than a mile now," Nina whispered. The
buildings, which had grown progressively shabbier,
were giving way to broken dirt roads and abandoned
fields. I could see the Endless Jungle in the distance,
sprawled wide and dark before us.

"Almost there," I murmured. Behind us, something
rustled, and Nina jumped, clutching my arm. "For
God's sake, Reya, you're giving me anxiety—"

"That wasn't me," I hissed. "And why are we whispering? We haven't seen any soldiers for *miles*—"

"But we definitely will if you keep up this racket—"

She fell silent so quickly, it was like she'd been
struck mute.

I turned around, mouth still open in retort, to see
the soldiers looming above us. Their horses whinnied
loudly, and I felt my skin go cold.

Their commander pulled off his helmet, and I realized that he was barely older than Nina. The fury in his purple eyes terrified me even more than the sword at his belt.

"What's your name?" he demanded.

We said nothing, and he bared his teeth. "Do you have any idea who I am?"

"No," I whispered, looking down.

The young commander dismounted, and I noticed the seal on his lapel. It was an ornate *Z*, carved with a royal insignia.

Z for Zakir.

"I'm Prince Devendra Zakir," the boy said coldly. "Heir to the throne and imperial commander of Kasmira. So I will ask you one more time, and you'd better answer: *What is your name?*"

Nina cleared her throat. "Deepa," she lied, but was betrayed by the tremor in her voice.

Behind us, horse hooves clattered. I turned to see a veiled female figure riding towards us, a short silver whip dangling from her fingers. Through a slit in her veil, her eyes landed on mine. They were golden and round, like a cat's.

"Well, Lady Sharati?" Devendra barked. I recoiled as the woman approached me, bending so close that I could feel her whip quivering in the breeze.

I heard her whisper something to me—words that were alien and eerie, but strangely familiar. I couldn't explain what happened next, but I felt an unearthly tingle beneath my skin, as if something within my blood was stirring. Instinctively, unequivocally, I knew what it was. Magic.

Lady Sharati was a Mage.

"Amar Kandhari's blood runs in her veins," she said harshly. "My magic does not lie, Prince Devendra. This is the Bookweaver."

Next to me, Nina stiffened. I had no idea what this Mage had done, but we had no time to dwell on it. I looked around wildly—there was nowhere to run.

The soldiers dismounted, and I heard the scrapes of swords leaving sheaths. "Nina Nadeer and Reya Kandhari," Devendra said, and I felt a jolt of fear at hearing my true name used at last. "You are wanted by my father, our glorious ruler Jahan, for treachery against the Zakir crown."

I was dimly aware of my heartbeat in my own ears.

Beside me, Nina's eyes had lost their characteristic defiance. She wasn't even afraid—she looked empty. The sight of her eyes sparked something deep within me.

Without thinking, I shoved Prince Devendra into Sharati, sending them both tumbling down the street. The soldiers lunged at me, but I was invincible. There was a roaring, rushing heat in my blood—a white-hot power that I had never felt before. And the magic erupted at once in a terrible scream, wrenching the flames from within my blood—

A reddish haze swirled around me, streaming acrid smoke—my magic had burst free with a primal vengeance. Streaming from me was fire, dark as the funeral pyres upon which we burned our dead, sacrificed our pride, purged our sins—

"Run!" I screamed at Nina, but it was the soldiers who obeyed my command. Carrying their prince, some scrabbling backwards on their knees, they rushed around the corner and out of sight. I lashed forward and they cowered, but I had no mercy for those who had killed my father—

Nina reached hesitantly for my hand.

At her touch, the flames melted back into my skin, and the world blinked back into focus. Suddenly, I was overcome by fatigue—my knees buckled, and Nina caught me just before I hit the ground.

The soldiers were regrouping, Devendra and Sharati stumbling to their feet, but I could not focus on that, not as spots of sun flickered before my eyes, causing Nina's face to shine and warp.

"Reya—Reya, come on, please get up, they're coming back!"

I struggled to focus on Nina's face. "Go," I muttered. "Too tired … just leave me here … "

She hefted me into her arms, and next thing I knew, Nina was sitting on top of Sharati's horse, and I was flung across the back, holding onto her shoulders like a child.

"Come on, move, horse—" Nina's voice was desperate as she tugged the reins. With an almighty lurch, the horse began a full charge forward into the blinding light.

Right before we hit the Jungle, I caught a glimpse of the soldiers in the alley, their spears glinting like a thousand tiny suns. My gaze landed squarely on Devendra's cold purple eyes. In spite of everything, I winked at him before I passed out.

Four

The first thing I was aware of was the rain, pelting the earth with silver needles.

I opened my eyes and saw the dappled silhouettes of leaves, framing an ashen sky. For a moment, I thought I had fallen from my mango tree, and the storms had unleashed themselves once more—

As the fog cleared, I realized that I was in a jungle, sheltered from the rain by the snarled branches of a banyan tree. To my right, I caught a glimpse of long black hair.

"Nina?"

She was at my side immediately. "How are you feeling?" Nina said gently.

I flexed my fingers experimentally, making sure they still worked. "I'm not dead," I managed.

Nina looked torn between laughing and yelling at me. Without warning, she crushed me with a hug.

"What was that for?" I said, rubbing my sore arms.

"You scared the life out of me," she said. "I checked your pulse. Your heart nearly stopped a few times."

Our eyes met, and in spite of everything, I laughed. She bit her lip, but then she smiled too. Because somehow, in that rainy jungle, we were both alive and together. For the moment, that was enough.

"I'll try not to do that again," I said. "But what happened to Devendra? Where are we?"

Nina frowned. "I don't know. The Mage's horse carried us out of the Raj and we rode for hours into the Endless Jungle."

I blinked. "Wait. We have a horse?"

Nina sighed. "It ran away—I have no idea. But Reya, how did you do that? I thought Devendra and his witch had caught us, but somehow you conjured fire to fight him off. I thought that Mages were extinct!"

It felt as though the ground had opened beneath me, yawning like oblivion. I had somehow conjured fire and burned the soldiers. I had used illegal magic.

"I—I'm not a Mage. I've never even met one before. I don't know how I did that. All I know is that they were hurting you, and ..."

I trailed off at the sight of Nina's face. She was staring at me with an expression I could not place, and I instinctively felt embarrassed. Did she think I was crazy? Was the look on her face fear, shock, disgust ... or was it awe?

"Well, whatever that was, it worked," she said at last. "I can't believe it. You're Reya Kandhari. You're the Bookweaver."

I wished she hadn't said that. After seven years in hiding, the sound of my name filled me with terror. It felt like all of my secrets had come undone, and everything I'd ever known was finally crashing down.

"Let's get out of here first," I said. "We need to find somewhere safe to spend the night."

Nina nodded. "You're right. Soldiers will be searching for us soon, if not already, and we're only a few hours' ride from the Raj."

We picked ourselves up and began to walk. "Where will we go?" Nina asked.

I looked up into the rippling afternoon sky. "As far as we can make it," I said. "We'll find somewhere to set up camp around sunset."

"That's not what I meant," said Nina. "Where are we running *to*? We can't hide in the Endless Jungle forever. Eventually, we'll need to find a new home."

She was right, of course. But the thought of my own vast and uncharted future was terrifying. It felt like peering over a cliff and seeing dark nothingness below.

Then I remembered what I hadn't before.

"I have my father's book of Kasmiri mythology!" I said. "It's bound to have a map in it."

I reached into my pocket and pulled out the book; Nina gasped when she saw it. Its gilded cover seemed to glimmer in the light.

I flipped through the pages until I found what I was looking for: the hand-painted map of Kasmira that spanned two pages. Landmarks sprang out at me—the Raj, cocooned within the Endless Forest. The city of Bharata beneath the Aharya mountains. Tahore, ensnarled by the sea. Varasi, pushing against the border with Indira.

Along the border was an inscription.

The ancient land of Kasmira is hewn from rugged jungle and mountains, bejeweled with historic cities. Its neighboring nation, Indira, has been at war with Kasmira since the beginning of the Zakir dynasty. Minor skirmishes constantly shift the border a mile east one day, two miles west the next. The border is a haven for refugees, because beyond the grip of the Zakir regime, freedom and anarchy reign.

"What do you think, Nina?"

I turned to see Nina staring resolutely away, her cheeks red. "Nina?"

"I can't read," she muttered.

I was too stunned to respond. I had forgotten that Nina, like most peasants, couldn't read. My father taught me to read before he taught me to walk, and it had always felt as natural as breathing. To think that nobody had ever bothered to teach Nina seemed incredibly unfair.

"I—okay," I said, not wanting to embarrass her. "Well, I think we're in the Endless Jungle. Here." I pointed it out on the map. "And to the west is the border with Indira. My father says it's a safe place for refugees seeking shelter from the king."

I closed the book. "Nina, how do you feel about going to Indira?"

Nina looked apprehensive. I didn't blame her. The thought of fleeing to another country, let alone Kasmira's sworn enemy, was dizzying.

"If it's far away from the Zakirs, I'm in," she said at last. "I just ... I never guessed it would come to this."

Guilt washed through me. Nina had given up everything to join me on this journey, and I was afraid that now, she was having second thoughts. It had always been my duty to survive, to uproot my life and detach from the past. But Nina wasn't used to the routine of secrets, fear, and impermanence.

"It's okay," said Nina, as though she was reading my mind. "We'll get through this. There's a new life waiting for us in Indira."

I nodded, still overcome by misgivings. "You're right. We'll use sunset tonight to find west, and then—"

"And then we find home," Nina finished. She took my hand, and together we trudged forward through the trees.

In the six hours that followed, I learned that hell is not burning hot or freezing cold.

It's not located deep beneath the earth, or guarded by demons in a great abyss in space. It's right here in Kasmira, thick and moist and suffocatingly green. It's filled with blood-sucking insects, screeching monkeys, and creeping vines.

Hell is a jungle, and we were in hell.

We had only just entered the Endless Jungle, but I could already appreciate the name. The paths were dark and identical, as they had been for the past six hours. Through the trees, I caught sight of sleeping cobras, fat lizards, even a herd of wild elephants.

Still, once I grew numb to the mosquitoes, I came to the grudging realization that the jungle was beautiful. Great trees soared like ancient wooden temples, the leafy altars forming canopies overhead.

When the day neared dusk, Nina and I set up camp near a stream. While Nina waded after the tigerfish, I scaled the nearby papaya trees. By the time Nina returned with the squirming fish, my pockets were plump with fruit.

A day ago, I would have turned down Nina's request to scoop tigerfish innards, but a single afternoon in the wild had already changed that.

"I feel like I've spent so long trying to survive," I confessed to Nina, "that maybe I forgot how to actually live."

Nina popped a fish gut between her fingers. "If this isn't the good life," she said, "I don't know what is." She caught my eye and laughed.

All of a sudden, I felt it.

It was like someone was watching me from behind—I could *feel* eyes on the back of my head. Except this time, somebody was watching me from within my mind: hovering at the edge of my thoughts, waiting, leading me deeper into the forest.

I heard Nina calling my name, and I could've easily turned back. But somehow, I knew that wherever I was going, I was meant to go. I could feel my presence all at once in a jungle full of presences as bright as mine. I would use the word *spirit* if I believed in that kind of thing, because something—*someone*—was guiding me.

I pushed aside a branch, and on the ground, I saw it.

Its majestic head was slumped to the side, as splendid in person as it had been in my father's folktales. The *airavat* slowly turned its neck so that its eyes could meet mine.

The winged elephant was wounded, but it glimmered nonetheless: not with light reflected from the dying sun, but somehow created by its very skin. Its milky wings were fluttering limply, and a gash along its trunk spilled blood, like ink drops on fresh paper.

"Nina?"

I knelt beside the *airavat*. My hands brushed tentatively against its elephantine forehead, but it did not shrink at my touch. I could feel its presence exploring mine, flitting but never touching, like two magnets' repelling ends. And in that moment, memories that weren't mine rushed through me.

It was like standing in front of a wave the moment before it breaks. I was overwhelmed with a staggering force, memories pulsing through me like water. *Grass and moonlight. Warm summer skies, soaring through the clouds, pushing against heaven itself. Tigers, claws slashing, roaring, falling—*

Nina found me a minute later, cradling the dead *airavat* with tears in my eyes.

"A white elephant. It's so beautiful," she whispered, gazing sadly at the *airavat*. "I thought all the mythical beasts had died out long ago. How did you find it?"

I looked away. "You're not going to believe me if I tell you," I said. "I felt its spirit calling me. I don't know. It's crazy."

"Maybe it's not," said Nina in hushed tones. "You're a Mage. You unlocked your powers. Maybe you can sense magic now."

We walked back to camp in silence as the sun's rays dimmed into blackness, stars sprinkled on an inky wash. We settled under an old banyan, and soon enough, Nina's deep breathing told me that I was the only one awake.

Actually, I wasn't.

I listened to the cries of peacocks, the splashes of tigerfish, and—maybe I was imagining it—the wing-beats of a thousand carefree *airavats* in the sky. Somehow, I wasn't alone. When the fire erupted, something had awoken in me, something vast and relentlessly beautiful. It was a quiet little infinity that I could only describe as *magic*.

I woke up to a golden sky.

It illuminated the rocks, the trees, the entire jungle. I imagined my father's writing brush cascading across the landscape, streaking new layers of watered ink.

Last night sparked a burning desire in me to learn more about who I was. Mages had been tabooed in society for seven years; I was sure they were extinct. Only now did I suspect that my father might have concealed just as much from me as he had from the outside world.

Maybe he couldn't speak to me, but I still had a piece of him left. I had an opening into the world he never shared with me.

I opened his book and began to read.

> *The powers of the Bookweaver were melded by the ancient Yogis, who were born as common Mages. Due to their ancestry, Bookweavers possess a rare duality of powers. The first is the power shared by all Mages: the ability to manipulate the world through magic. However, the second power belongs to only Bookweavers, created by the first Bookweaver himself. It is called*

vayati: *the art of weaving the Bookweaver's words into reality.*

Ancient laws of magic govern the art of vayati. *The gods ordain that in order to perform* vayati, *the Bookweaver must have awakened his Yogi state. Thus,* vayati *requires enormous will-power and meditation, and most Bookweavers only achieve the Yogi state once in their lifetime after intense preparation.*

Like all Mages, Bookweavers are limited by the physical toll of their magic. A spell too tremendous could cause the death of the Bookweaver. Unless that Bookweaver has produced an heir or transferred the Gift to another, this would result in a dead-end in the line of Yogis, disrupting the balance of Kasmira.

My fingers shook as I closed the book.

I nearly died practicing magic yesterday. Now I understood why.

"You look concerned."

I turned to see that Nina had woken without my notice. I smiled at her. "How'd you sleep?"

She shrugged. "For some strange reason, whenever I closed my eyes, I kept imagining creepy Mage-ladies chasing me on horseback." I laughed, and we started packing up our camp.

Nina set out to fill the waterskin while I cooked the remaining tigerfish, counting on the early morning mist to conceal the smoke. I could hear Nina splashing softly; it occurred to me that at some point, I was going to need a bath.

And then I heard it—horse hooves, thundering

impossibly fast, quickening the beat of my pulse. Silently, my lips formed Nina's name.

Devendra had found us again.

Five

Deep down, my instincts must have kicked in, because within seconds, I grabbed our things and started running.

Adrenaline pulsed through my veins as I charged past the trees, legs pumping faster than I ever thought possible. A sharp branch caught me across the forehead, but I barely felt it. All I could register was the crackle of leaves beneath my feet, the beat of horse hooves, the chortle of the stream where Nina was defenseless—

I raced towards Nina, tripped, and crashed facefirst into the river. By the sheer momentum of my still-pumping legs, I managed to stay afloat before Nina hauled me upright.

"Devendra," I managed, still spluttering. "He's here."

It was like her instincts kicked in, too—Nina immediately tugged me towards the other side of the river. We ducked behind the overgrown reeds sprouting from the water.

"Where is he?" Nina's voice was almost impossible to hear. She had crouched so low in the water that only her head was visible.

"They're all nearly at our clearing," I breathed.

She cursed softly. "The wood. Is it still burning?"

"No, thank the gods," I whispered. "I stamped it out—but our food is still there."

Nina groaned. "In that case," she breathed, "our only chance is that they'll think we're already gone."

I felt my adrenaline slowly ebb away, but then a voice drifted through the woods.

"The Kandhari girl has been here. Look at that tigerfish. It's still smoking."

Devendra's voice, cold and stinging, sent a shiver down my spine. We'd barely escaped him the first time. Now, I wasn't sure that I could take him again.

"There are two sets of footprints," he continued. "She's still traveling with Nina Nadeer."

Nina gave a slight start at the sound of her name.

A horse neighed impatiently. "Someone silence the horses," Devendra demanded. There was shuffling, and the horses were silent.

"How did they escape us again?" said a harsh female voice. Nina and I exchanged glances of alarm: the voice belonged to Lady Sharati, the veiled Mage who'd identified me in the Raj.

Clearly, today was not our day.

"Commander, this is your soldiers' fault," snarled Sharati. "If they'd kept the horses silent, the girls wouldn't have heard us coming. They're probably running right now." She huffed. "First your failure with Kandhari's fire magic, and now this. It's no wonder King Jahan nearly disowned you—"

Devendra interrupted sharply. "The imperial soldiers aren't to blame. And don't you dare mention my father. I *will* regain his favor."

"That remains to be seen. You'll be lucky if you're still imperial commander after this," Sharati said coolly.

"Shut up." Devendra's voice was low. "Why aren't you using magic to find them, Mage?"

"I don't know where they're located, so I can't direct my powers at them," said Sharati. "But I can direct them at *your soldiers* if they don't start searching!"

Devendra's voice, tight with annoyance, rang through the trees. "And risk failing my father? The girl is his utmost priority. And now that she's unlocked her powers, there's no way we're defeating her without magic."

There was a heavy pause.

"All right, Zakir," said Sharati. "I'll try."

Her voice grew deadly soft. I could barely hear her words, only fragments of a powerful language that sent chills down my spine.

"Vindati... nivista... vyada ..."

A breath of warm wind swept over us and then subsided.

There was a crash in the forest. "My lady?" began Prince Devendra, but he was met with silence.

"Maybe Sharati's dead," someone said. "That magic must've tired her out."

I couldn't believe my luck. Evidently, neither could Devendra.

"She's fainted," said the crown prince. "We ought to leave the hag here, for all she's worth. Except my father would be furious. I don't know why he relies on these Mage freaks."

Nina met my eye. It was time to go, while Devendra was busy figuring out what to do. Slowly—afraid of making so much as a rustle—we untangled ourselves from the reeds and waded across the bank. We scrabbled onto dry land, and then we ran, our wet clothes like weights on our bodies. Nina was at my side, sprinting so fast she was a blur of dark hair.

I was exhausted by the time Nina finally slowed to a halt, clothes fully dried. My breath was ragged, and my heartbeat felt like an elephant dancing on my chest. Without warning, my knees gave way.

Nina caught me before I hit the jungle floor. She, too, was bent over, breathing hard from the exertion.

"We need to keep moving," she said. "We're only a few miles from our old camp." She glanced at the scrape on my face from the branch. "We have to do something about that. You're still bleeding."

I leaned back as she set to work, tearing a strip from a shirt. She wrapped it tightly around my forehead, and I glanced at my reflection in the flat side of the knife. My short hair stuck up in all directions, and my face was covered in dirt, making it appear as though I'd suddenly tanned.

"That was way too close," Nina said. "How did they find us?"

I took a deep breath. "I don't know. But there's a squadron of soldiers, the crown prince, and a Mage on their side, so it's only a matter of time until they find us again. We're outnumbered in the jungle."

Nina closed her eyes, thinking. "You're right. They're on horseback, so there's no chance we can outrun them, at least not through the jungle."

She looked at me, and her eyes lit up. "You know,

maybe we've been thinking about this all wrong.
Hiding in the forest—we're too easy to track. Maybe
we're better off hiding in plain sight. In a city."

I wasn't so sure. "The cities will be filled with soldiers," I pointed out.

"But they're so crowded, we have a chance of
going unnoticed," said Nina. "We're getting nowhere
on foot. If we can make it to a city, we can stock up
on supplies, steal a horse. Either way, we need to
move fast."

She was right, of course. I pulled out the map and
scanned it quickly.

"Since we're going west, we'll pass by Bharata," I
said, reading through my father's notes. "It's the sec-
ond-biggest city in Kasmira after the Raj. It says here
that my father grew up there," I added, surprised.

Nina squeezed my hand. "Then it's decided," she
said. "I've always wanted to see Bharata."

The bright noon gave way to long afternoon shadows; we kept walking until it was dark. We set up
camp near a jungle cave, but didn't dare light a fire; I
shivered in the cold night breeze.

Nina gave me a sideways look. "I've been on the
run with you for two days and I still don't know
enough about you," she said. "The real you, anyways."

I hesitated. Memories had become painful to me,
but this was Nina. I took a deep breath and let the
words weave themselves.

*For as long as she could remember, her life had
been shaped by words. Words of mystique and*

mythology. Words of magic that glowed like candles in her heart. Words that transformed the Bookweaver into the living legacy of his ancestors. Words of promise that wove themselves into her destiny.

The Bookweaver's daughter was raised by a village, built by her loving mother, who taught her to be strong, and her powerful father, who instilled magic in her blood. Grandparents, uncles, even cousins she no longer played with. Her family name was strong, but her heritage was stronger, and the ancestors guarded over her each night.

She grew up in her father's library, climbing the bookshelves to watch the distinguished guests—Mages traveling from lands across the desert. Writers and sorcerers and warriors and princes. She especially liked the king, Viraj, because he brought her gifts: a peacock quill, an astrolabe, and on festival days, a book.

It was close to her eighth birthday when things began to change. Tension rippled through the streets—a darkness on the edge of town. At night, the girl heard crackling and burning outside the house—enough fire to fill a thousand suns. There was one name her parents kept repeating: Zakir. It sounded like a curse.

The king stopped visiting. Her father was solemn for days. It worried her to see her father like that, but she wasn't truly afraid, not until the night all the windows broke in her house. There was an explosion of sound, like glass had turned to rain. When it was over, she rushed down the stairs.

There stood the Bookweaver, covered in blood, but her mother was nowhere in sight.

That night, visitors arrived with hushed voices and mournful faces. They told her that her mother had joined the warm and wonderful realm of the ancestors. And while the girl was comforted, she couldn't help but wonder why her mother couldn't have taken her along.

She fled in the dark of night, following the Bookweaver to a dingy hut. She shed her name, Kandhari, and assumed a new name, Patel. She soon learned that it was one thing to read fiction, and quite another to live it. She wove lies into tapestries of secrets, but the problem with fiction is that if left unchecked, it comes true.

It comes true.

Nina had tears in her eyes when I finished. "Reya," she said. "I'm sorry."

I couldn't meet her eyes. "I've made my peace with it," I said. "So did my father."

She squeezed my arm. "The moment I met you, I could tell you weren't an orphan," she said.

I stared at her. "How?"

Nina shrugged. "They—*we*—orphans can tell each other apart. When nobody's loved you, it shows. You can see it in our eyes," she said. "But you? You were loved. I never knew your father, but I know he loved you. You were lucky."

I looked away.

"I don't know," I said. "Maybe never knowing and

never hurting is better than loving and losing." I was irritated to feel tears stinging my eyes, and I fought to keep my voice even. "Because God knows that losing him, it hurts."

Nina sighed. "How did you get through it, losing your parents?" I asked her. "How *do* you get through it?"

She shrugged. "Some people say you can't," she said. "But that can't be true. I don't believe that you get a one-shot chance at being loved, and if they die, it's over. I mean, I hardly remember my parents anyways, and maybe you're right, maybe I am better off that way. But I promise you, it will stop hurting eventually. It has to."

I nodded. "Right now, it just doesn't feel real. It feels like tomorrow we'll be back home and my father will be waiting for me. It's just … my father was my anchor, and I don't know who I am without him."

She smiled sideways at me, and I hastily wiped my eyes. "Reya, listen to me. You're going to find yourself again. We'll find it together in Indira."

"You can be my new family," I told her. "We'll be like a sisterhood of orphans."

"The sorority of the depressed and disillusioned." Nina smiled. "You can be our mascot."

Six

We walked until we could see the Aharya Mountains, coated in swirling mist. They could have belonged in one of my father's myths—alluring and boundless, promising adventure and a hint of melancholy.

"The mountains are breathtaking," murmured Nina. "I've never seen anything so massive, not even the *mahal.*"

Even though we were still miles away, the Aharyas were so tall that we could barely see the peaks.

"They make me feel small," Nina continued quietly, tracing my father's map with reverence. "This journey makes me think—well, there's so much out there. Mountains and cities and rivers, entire chapters full of legacies over generations…"

Her fingers ran, almost unconsciously, against the embossed cover. "Someday, I hope I can learn to read."

As I looked at her, I imagined my life if *I* couldn't read. It occurred to me that as Bookweaver, I could do so much. I could teach a thousand girls like Nina to read—a magic more potent than anything a Mage could summon. It was a hopeful thought.

But the hope didn't last long, because at some point, we became painfully aware of the growls coming from deep within our stomachs. We hadn't found anything edible all day.

I carefully rationed the fibrous innards I had scooped from a jute tree—an old trick I learned from my father.

Nina took her portion gratefully. "Remember the barley *naan* in the Fields?" she asked between mouthfuls.

"Even week-old *naan* bread sounds delicious now," I agreed. "And potatoes—God, potato curry—sautéed in butter and spices."

She laughed. "Forget the peasant food. What I really want is meat. Glistening, juicy, and well-seasoned meat."

"You know, I've always wanted to quit eating meat," I said. "It's not like I could afford the butcher's anyway, but I would like to minimize the pain I inflict on the world. I mean, we've been exploited all our lives. Why do the same to animals?"

Nina shook her head. "Sometimes you're too noble for your own good," she said, smirking.

I was about to retort when I suddenly caught a scent quite separate from the earthy jute. Clearly wafting through the jungle was a smoky aroma—heavy, succulent.

Nina's head turned with a swiftness that reminded me of a hound on the scent. "Is it just me?" she whispered.

I shook my head, my stomach already dancing with excitement. Food meant human proximity, which could be dangerous, but I was too hungry to think straight. Together, we crept in the direction of the smell.

In the clearing before us stood a cluster of empty tents. Between them, I could see what looked like a full boar, roasting serenely in a pit of coals. The camp was silent except for the rustling of tents in the wind.

"I can't believe this," said Nina. She blinked slowly. "Maybe the hunger has messed with our minds and this is a grand hallucination."

I was already striding past the empty tents. "Come on, Nina. Our dinner's getting cold."

We wasted no time preparing the food—we pulled the meat apart with our bare hands. I had just taken my first bite when Nina suddenly gasped.

"Wait a minute," she demanded. "What happened to inflicting less pain on the world?"

I glared at her and she laughed, a little too hard. "Shut up and eat, or I'll inflict pain on you," I warned.

We went through the tents to steal much-needed supplies before the camp's occupants returned. I gleefully traded my dirty bamboo shoes for sturdy boots. Whoever stayed here obviously lived off the land—I unearthed compasses, water skins, and even a bow.

I'd never shot a bow in my life, but in Nina's hands, this bow could be a valuable tool.

"Nina?" I called.

She didn't respond, so I dragged the bow into the silent clearing. For a second, I was alone except for the rustling of old trees.

Then I saw Nina. She was standing so still, she looked rooted to the earth. Her eyes were fixed on the sword resting against her throat.

Gripping its handle was a young woman who loomed over Nina, her eyes glinting like steel. A group of people had suddenly appeared, as if they'd grown out of the jungle itself. My hands flew to the bow that I didn't think I knew how to use. I notched an arrow.

"Put the bow down," said the woman.

I hesitated, and she jostled Nina closer to the sword, causing her to gasp.

My heart hammered as I lowered the bow to the ground.

"I'm sorry," I said. "I don't know who you are, but I don't want any trouble. Please let her go."

The woman laughed. "She talks like a city girl, with all the pleases and thank yous," she said to her armed companion, who also chuckled. She dropped Nina unceremoniously to the ground. "Little girl, I think you asked for trouble the minute you laid waste to my boar. I don't take kindly to thieves. I ought to turn you in."

"That's funny," I said. "Do all thieves have such straightlaced morals, or is it just you?"

Nina's eyes were wide. She shook her head frantically, clearly warning me to shut up.

I pressed on recklessly. "Because from what I've seen—the traveling camp, the weapons, the suspicious goods—I'm guessing that you're not going to turn us in. In fact, I'm willing to bet that you're in even more trouble with the law than we are."

I didn't know where my sudden courage was coming from, but I was staring the woman in the eye. She appraised me, but she no longer looked threatening. She wore a strange expression—was it shock, amusement, or pity?

"Thieves' honor," she said. "From the looks of you,

you haven't been a fugitive for more than a week. So I'm going to teach you the first rule: you never steal from another thief."

"Noted," I said. "Now, if you let us go, we'll be gone."

The woman raised her eyebrows. "I don't think so. You'll be dead in a fortnight on your own. And since I like you, I think you'd better stay with us for a while."

She sheathed her sword and Nina lurched towards me. I followed the woman before she could change her mind.

Her companion led us silently to seats around the fire, handing us plates of food. We gulped it down hastily, too terrified to do anything else within arm's length of his sword.

"Why are you helping us?" I asked at last.

The woman glanced up at us from the knife she was polishing.

"That's a funny thing to ask," she said. "Second rule of fugitive life: don't question your meals. You never know when you'll get another one."

"Lay off them, Aisha," said the young man next to her. He smiled at us. "My name's Niam Chori, and Aisha is my sister. We're helping you because we look out for our own. I don't know who you are, but anyone who's hiding from Jahan Zakir is a friend of ours."

Nina and I exchanged glances. "So everyone in this camp is on the run from the king?" said Nina. "You've been fugitives for the last seven years?"

Niam Chori shrugged. "Some of us. Aisha and I lost our parents when they got caught harboring Mages. Aran here," he added, nodding at the silent man who had fed us, "was a spy on the royal Council before he was caught. Jahan didn't let him forget it."

Aran nodded gravely, and I realized he was mute. The king had taken his voice.

I turned back to Aisha and Niam. "You're the resistance," I said. "You stood up for the Mages and the Yogis when they were being driven out of the country."

Aisha nodded. "Officially, we're the Renegades," she said. "We're headed to Bharata to meet up with the rest of our forces. Rumor has it that there's still one Yogi alive in Kasmira. And we're going to find her before the king does."

I could practically hear Nina's heart thumping beside me.

Niam smiled. "So that's our story. What about yours?"

Nina looked at me, and I could almost read her thoughts. It was dangerous to reveal ourselves to anyone, no matter who they were. But on the other hand, we stood little chance on our own, playing the game of survival without even knowing the rules.

She nodded imperceptibly—we agreed.

"I have a feeling that your search for the last Yogi is about to get a lot shorter," I managed.

Niam's eyes widened, and the gravity of my words registered on his face. "I'm Reya Kandhari," I said, confirming his look of dawning shock. "I'm the Bookweaver's daughter."

Out of the corner of my eye, I saw Nina's muscles tighten in preparation to fight or flee. But all around me, the Renegades did something unexpected. Not all at once—some led by Niam, some of their own accord, some caught up in the movement of the crowd around them—they sunk to their knees before me, a river rippling in the wind.

Niam Chori glanced up at me, awe in his eyes. "Bookweaver," he said. "It's been seven long years. Welcome back."

Aisha stood and embraced me. I felt my nerves relax at her touch, but I still felt thoroughly bewildered.

"Niam—why did everyone just—" I indicated the entire body of the Renegades, still kneeling. Niam nodded and the Renegades rose, resuming their duties with respectful salutes in our direction.

"They're loyal to you, Bookweaver," he said quietly. "You're too young to remember, but the Yogis have long protected the common people in our ranks. To see you, alive and well ... to many of us, you're the first sign of hope in a long time."

Nina and I followed the Choris through the camp. My mind was overflowing with questions, and I seized onto one at random.

"How have you survived all these years?" I asked. "I had no idea the resistance was still strong under Jahan's nose."

Aisha smiled heavily. "We barely survived," she said. "There was a huge royal crackdown after you escaped, which forced our entire Bharata regiment to go underground. But we owe it to your dad that we even made it this far," she added, nodding to me. "I'm sorry to hear about him, by the way."

My breath caught in my throat. "You knew my father?"

Niam nodded. "The Kandharis took care of us during their height of power," he said. "Amar—and all the Yogis, for that matter—protected the poor. When things got dangerous, while he still could, he smuggled a lot of intelligence that kept us alive. He was a brave man."

There was a moment of silence, and I was grateful to Nina for filling it, because my throat had choked up.

"What do you know about the king?" she asked. "There's no way we can escape him without knowing what he's up to."

Aisha's eyebrows contracted. "As of yesterday, there are wanted posters of you in every city. Parts of the Raj are on lockdown," she said. "The king's moving fast. We don't have time to smuggle you away."

Nina nodded. "He sent the crown prince on our trail," she told Aisha, who exchanged troubled glances with her brother.

"Prince Devendra?" she asked. I nodded in response. "Do you know him?" I said.

Niam sighed. "Unfortunately, we do. He's the reason Aran doesn't have much to say."

Aran grimaced, and my eyes widened. "But he's only—"

"Sixteen," finished Aisha. "I know. But Devendra is a Zakir. He's a military genius and the imperial commander of Kasmira, and he's been ruthless in tracking down insubordination. Always trying to please his twisted father."

"His father?"

"Word is that Devendra was nearly disowned when he let you escape the Raj," explained Niam. "Capturing you is the only way he regains royal favor. He will do anything—kill anyone—for it."

Nina looked at me grimly.

"So what can we do?" I asked. "We need help, but not if it means endangering the Renegades. We're up against the might of imperial Kasmira, and people could get hurt."

Niam grinned.

"That's noble of you," he said. "But we've been evading the king for a very long time. If we can bring you to Bharata, it'll be pretty damn hard for Jahan to pin you down."

Unfamiliar emotions were wrestling inside me—anxiety, joy, gratitude. It took me a moment to identify what I was feeling: relief.

"Thank you," I managed. "I don't know how I could repay you for this."

Aisha's expression was fierce.

"Just don't die," she said. "There are a lot of hopes riding on you, and a lot of people who have been oppressed for far too long. They need you to prove that resistance is still possible."

Niam gave me a reassuring pat on the shoulder. "Onward to Bharata?" he offered. And in spite of everything, I smiled.

Seven

It's hard to express the chasm between loneliness and having allies. It was more than just strength in numbers—there was something about the Renegades that made me feel like my pain could be part of something greater. Like my father's legacy could mean something at last.

Nina settled in well. When we weren't on the move, she was busy—sparring with Aisha, helping Aran on scouting trips. I was relieved to see her smile again. She joined me in our tent one evening, holding my father's book.

"Reya," she said. "I've been thinking about it, and I'm finally ready to learn how to read."

"That's amazing, Nina," I said. "But what changed your mind?"

As far as I knew, Nina hated anything intellectual—for her whole life, education had been a luxury she could never afford. Tragic circumstances had caused her to rank literacy far below every other priority for survival.

"I'm not sure," she admitted. "I've just been listening to the Renegades' stories, and I realized how much we're exploited because of our ignorance. For the past seven years, I hated Mages like you, just because I didn't know anything about them. Does that make sense?"

I nodded, and Nina continued. "And I think being able to read will let me make decisions for myself. I won't be a slave to whatever the king wants me to believe."

"Okay," I said. "How are you going to learn?"

For a moment, there was silence, and I realized that Nina was staring at me expectantly.

My cheeks burned. "Wait—*me?* You want me to teach you?"

Nina rolled her eyes. "Who else?" she said. "But relax. I'm extremely smart, even if you're a stupid teacher."

I laughed. "Shut up," I said. "We'll start with the alphabet."

I found a piece of parchment in my bag, rolled around my father's delicate silver quill. Carefully, I inked a clear letter *A* on the page.

"See this?" I asked Nina. She stared at it with almost painful concentration, like she was trying to imprint it in her brain. "It looks like an arrow head," she noted.

"Actually, yeah," I said, surprised. "*A* is the first letter in *arrow.*"

She took the quill and drew a rickety *A* on the sheet. Her hand shook slightly, and she looked to me for approval.

"Not bad," I said. But Nina could always tell when I was lying.

"Really?"

"A dying mongoose could do better," I admitted, "but you'll get there." I reached out and corrected her grip on the nib.

Nina flexed her wrist experimentally.

"This feels weird," she said. "It feels like a weapon, even though it's so fragile. It's beautiful."

She gave me a fleeting grin, and I looked at the new *A* she had produced. It was firm and hard, the kind no enemy wants to be shot with.

The days passed quickly. Daylight hours were spent on the march, and we got used to carrying our belongings as we walked, Renegade-style. Nina and I wove words by candlelight, Bharata looming closer with each successive night.

One night, we were reading beside the campfire when a group of Renegades returned from their scouting trip. Their voices were quiet, of course—fugitives do not have the luxury of loudness—but there was something heavy in the air.

Niam raised a hand, and the conversations died at once. "I have news," he said.

Nina and I turned to face Niam. Although he couldn't have been older than thirty, he looked ancient in the firelight—it accentuated the scars of hardship on his face, making him look leaner, tougher, harsh.

He sighed. "We just learned that our brothers and sisters in Tahore were discovered by imperial soldiers last night. I don't know exactly what happened to them, but we lost nearly forty comrades."

The camp was silent except for the crackling of flames. Niam pulled a flask from the depths of his cloak and drank. Then he passed it to me.

The alcohol burned as it slid down my throat. Immediately I felt invigorated, a little warmer. I passed the flask to Nina.

I listened quietly as Niam spoke, watching the flask go around the fire. There was something about him that reminded me of my father, and I took another strong swig to loosen the lump in my throat.

"There are many ways to be brave today," he said. "It can mean giving up what you love for your cause. It can mean sacrificing your life for something greater, like our friends in Tahore." He paused, and I could hear the rawness in his silence.

"But tonight, bravery is none of those things. Tonight is about holding our tears, clenching our fists, and marching forward despite the pain. That—" Niam's voice broke. "That is the bravery we need tonight while we mourn."

Aisha opened her mouth and began to sing, and following her lead, the Renegades joined in softly. It was an alluring, heroic song, echoed in all layers of voices, gritty and light. It was a song of joy and poetry, jarring strangely with the weight of grief.

Afterwards, the Renegades left, one by one, until only Nina and I sat around the dying fire with the Choris. Niam drank alone, Aisha's hand gentle on his shoulder. For the first time, he looked nothing like the strong, capable leader I'd known him to be.

Cautiously, Nina spoke. "That was a beautiful song, Aisha."

Aisha nodded. "It's a Kasmiri funeral song we sang

when I was in the army—that is, before the army was filled with mindless slaves of the Zakirs."

"But it's so happy," I said, before I could stop myself.

For the first time that evening, Aisha smiled.

"It's not the words that make it a funeral song, Reya," she said. "It's remembering who you used to sing it with. Eventually, you'll understand."

I found my voice again. "I know that being a Renegade is dangerous," I said. Niam glanced at me.

"Of course," he replied.

I took a deep breath.

"Niam, you're going through a lot, and I put you in more danger every day. If you wanted to split up, I'd understand. I don't want to hurt any of you."

Next to me, Nina nodded, affirming my words. I felt a rush of affection towards her.

Niam leaned forward to warm his hands over the fire.

"I'm going to let you in on a trade secret, Bookweaver," he said. "There's no space for fear or regret if you're going to be a warrior. Fighting a battle is like winning a game of *mancala*. From the moment you move the first shell, every move is deliberate. You cannot feel."

He hesitated. "Not with your head, anyways. You feel what you're fighting for—you feel that in your heart."

Niam finally looked away from the flames to meet my eyes. "So no, we're not leaving you. Our duty is to protect you. It would be poor repayment to Tahore's sacrifice if we abandoned you now."

We subsided into comfortable silence. Grief over my father was hitting me in waves, but somehow, it felt as though being part of the Renegades was holding it at bay. Even if they couldn't touch my individual agony, they had felt something that cut just as deeply. In our pain, we were united.

Eight

The next day, we were on the move once more.

The valley of the Aharyas at sunrise was like nothing I had ever imagined. Cool gold sunrays suffused the treetops, and rosy light deepened across the valleys, as though the mountains themselves were kindling.

Next to me, Aisha looked entranced. "In the mountains, nothing is ever as it seems," she told me. "I've been traveling these paths for seven years, but the Aharyas seem to change a little every time."

Nina's eyes were wide as she took in the sunrise. She, too, looked more carefree than I had ever seen her.

"I feel like Jahan has been around for so long, I forgot what life was like before him," Nina said. "I forgot there was something before him, and there will be something after."

She was right. As the sun rose higher in the sky, spiky purple shadows crept across the crags of the

Aharyas. There was something almost religious about the scene that left me completely dazzled.

"Mountains help you remember," I noted quietly. "They force you to realize how fleeting your problems are by confronting you with massive spans of time."

"It makes you question your own mortality, doesn't it?" Nina said, smiling a little. "It's humbling."

Aisha laughed. "You're awfully philosophical for a pair of fugitives," she said.

Abruptly, she stopped, and I immediately realized why.

Blocking the winding path before us was an enormous wave of fallen rocks and uprooted trees. The Renegades slowed to a halt, crowding along the path.

Niam joined us. "Just our luck," he said. "A landslide. These must have been uprooted by last week's monsoon. It's going to take half the day to clear the rocks."

The other Renegades dropped their travel packs and set to work. Aran joined us, looking worried. Niam patted his arm reassuringly. "It's only a minor setback," he said. "We haven't seen the royal soldiers in a week." Aran still looked uneasy, but he turned to help with the clearing effort. Nina and I followed him.

A knot of Renegades was hauling a massive tree trunk off the path. I marveled at the efficiency at which they worked, coordinating their movements, like soldiers in a well-trained army. Aran silently passed me a machete, pointing to a large cluster of branches.

I took the machete and started sawing at the gnarliest branch, Nina holding it taut for me. To my surprise, the branch was rubbery soft; green sap spewed from beneath the blade. I stopped and frowned, wiping my brow.

"What's wrong?" Nina asked.

"It's just—I've been working on trees for the past seven years," I said. "See this green sap? It means this is a healthy tree. There's no way it was uprooted by last week's monsoon."

Nina's eyes widened, and without warning, she released the branch, causing it to snap back into my face. "*Nina!*" I complained, but she was already running.

I followed her to the tree's base, which was being lifted onto a harness by the Renegades. And there, at the bottom of the tree, were the unmistakable sap-filled grooves, as if carved from my very machete.

These trees hadn't been uprooted last week. They had been cut, and not too long ago.

Nina and I stared at each other, and the enormity of our discovery caused my stomach to plunge. Without another word, we were running to where Niam and Aisha stood, surveying the damage.

"We need to get out of here," I panted. "This wasn't a landslide. Someone cut the trees and blocked the path. They're trying to trap us on the mountainside. The king knows where we're headed."

Niam's eyes widened, and he scrambled to collect his things. "I should've known," he hissed. He raised his voice, calling out to the Renegades scattered around the rubble. "Everyone, abandon the effort!" he shouted. "We've been compromised. Let's go!"

His words were drowned out by an awful explosion.

The blinding flash imprinted into my retinas—then my feet left the ground and I was hurtling backward as the impact took its toll.

We rolled out of sight into the brush below the path, and Niam glanced back at us, miraculously still standing, his eyes wide in horror. I struggled to get up, despite my dizziness, but I couldn't—Nina had landed on top of me. Instead, I could only look up helplessly at the avalanche of boulders, crushing the path before our eyes.

Then Devendra Zakir appeared, silhouetted against the rocks, and my fists clenched with hatred.

"Niam and Aisha Chori," he said coldly. "Your time has come."

As he spoke, figures emerged from the smoky gloom, until he was flanked by a full battalion, armed with explosives and weapons. They descended from the cliff, surrounding the Renegades.

I felt my heart pulsing in my throat. We'd been ambushed.

Nina helped me to my feet. From within the brush, we saw the remaining Renegades struggling to regroup, pulling their weapons out of the rubble, helping their wounded comrades. But it was painfully clear that they were already overwhelmed—the battle had already been lost.

I started to climb out of the brush, but Nina caught my arm. Her eyes were glazed with tears. "Don't, Reya," she whispered. "They're going to be defeated. The only way you survive is if you stay hidden."

I tugged against her grasp, but she wouldn't budge. "I can't stand and watch the Renegades die!" I hissed.

"Reya, please," said Nina. She was crying now. "Remember what Aisha said? You need to stay alive. If you don't, every Renegade died in vain."

I couldn't tell you what happened next. It's difficult to describe fractured visions of moments where there's nothing to make sense of, nothing except cruelty against those who wanted to protect you. It's like a song you can't quite remember; occasionally, you hear a rhythm of explosion, a ringing hiss, whispers of ash that dissolve into earth.

I buried my face into Nina's shoulder, trying my hardest to drown out the losing battle on the rocks above. "We know that the Bookweaver is traveling with you!" I heard Devendra yell.

Niam's voice rang out over the chaos. "We don't know where she is!" he said. "I'd start by searching under the rocks. Maybe you should've checked your aim before you blew up half the damn mountain."

Niam knew exactly where we were. He was trying to save our lives.

"Don't play with me, Chori." Devendra's voice was dangerous. "I've spent my life eradicating filthy Renegades. I will not hesitate to scourge you, as well."

In spite of everything, Niam laughed.

"Is that so, little boy?" he said, and I wanted to scream at Niam to stop goading Devendra, but Nina's hand was over my mouth. "Tell me, *Commander,* how's your dear father? What will he say when he realizes you've blown up the Bookweaver?"

"Shut up," said Devendra, but his hand was shaking. "Where's the girl?" He pointed his sword threateningly at Aisha, making the smile disappear from Niam's face.

It occurred to me that beneath the face of a sixteen-year-old boy, Devendra might be completely insane.

"I don't know," spat Niam. "Go ahead, kill us all, you—"

Devendra punched him across the face before he could finish his sentence.

For a moment, before Niam was dragged away by the soldiers, our eyes met. His lips formed words that I could barely hear over the shouts—"*The Flying Tiger!*"

There was no time to look back—Nina's voice was in my ear. "We need to run while they're distracted. Come on."

I nodded. The sunrise sky was blotted with smoke and dust. Our friends were being taken prisoner by the prince who had dogged us across the country.

Numbly, I tumbled down the side of the mountain with Nina at my side.

If the mountains could see, they would open their eyes to behold two desperate strangers, their awe of the view cloaked by horror beneath the red-tinged sky. The mountains, which had observed glorious sunrises long before Jahan's reign, stood unfeeling. They were irreverent, unconcerned by the battle that had just been lost.

As I ran, all I could think about was what Nina had said about the mountains being humbling. She was right. I had never felt as small as I did in that minute.

Nine

When we finally staggered over the mountain's crest, Bharata sprawled before us, branching like veins through the valley. Tears ran freely down Nina's face, but my eyes remained completely dry. I was numb.

Or maybe by that point, I was used to death. I'm not sure.

At last, Nina spoke. "What do you think Niam was trying to tell us?"

"What?"

She sighed. "He said a name before they arrested him. *The Flying Tiger.* Who is that?"

I shook my head. "I have no idea. Maybe it's a code name. Maybe it's someone who can help us find the Renegades in Bharata."

We couldn't be sure, of course. Because Niam Chori was gone.

At last the trees parted, and before us loomed the gates of Bharata. We melted into the crowd passing through the massive arches, and we were in.

Right away, I knew this was no place for a girl from the Fringes.

Bharata was a city of unthinkable dimensions, stretching wide and dizzyingly high, and I wanted to see it all.

A huge bazaar, erupting with color, bustled before us, its chaos contrasted by the hulking clock tower of the legendary Red Temple. Purple banners with the Zakirs' iconic *Z* waved cheerfully overhead.

We waded through the crowded bazaar. Children raced after a tiger cub with a bow around its neck, cutting an empty path through the traffic that was quickly filled by the next surge of people. Nina grabbed me before I could be crushed by a harried-looking woman with a monkey in her arms, a milk jug on her head, and a herd of chickens pecking at her feet.

"Stay with me," she whispered. "All of these people are making me anxious."

As if on cue, an imperial soldier peered out from the tallest turret of the Red Temple, and my stomach did a little flip. "Don't look now, but we've got company," I muttered. "Let's get the hell out of here."

I pulled my cloak over my eyes, and Nina did the same. As we shoved our way uptown, I noticed that the city was beginning to change: the buildings got shabbier, the sunlight gave way to shadows, and rats scurried at the sound of our footsteps. Clearly, this was the part of Bharata that visitors didn't see.

"Reya, look at this!" Nina said abruptly.

I followed her gaze to the wall before us, and my eyes widened.

Every inch of the wall was painted in thick, colorful strokes. Up close, it looked like a disorderly tangle of lines, but when Nina and I stepped back, a painting bloomed into view. It was unmistakable—bright green eyes, easy smile, flyaway mane of hair. The artist had captured him perfectly, and the sight of my father's face gutted me.

Below his portrait was an inscription. Nina's brow furrowed in concentration as she sounded the letters out.

"Amar Kandhari lives on," she read aloud. She turned to me, eyes shining in wonder. "This is beautiful, Reya," she said. "It's a monument to your father."

For a minute, I was too stunned to respond.

"Who would do this?" I said at last. Nina shrugged, but her voice was filled with awe.

"Niam did say that this place was a stronghold for the resistance," she said. "But whoever did this has guts. This is propaganda against the king."

I looked again at the painting with new eyes. Nina was right: this was a commemoration of my father. People were willing to risk treason to honor him. He was no longer just a ghost of my past: he was a symbol of hope. He was a martyr.

"Wait," Nina said. "What's that?"

I looked closer and noticed what I hadn't before: the corner of my father's finger, painted so hastily I had mistaken it for a smudge. It was pointing somewhere behind us.

Slowly, we turned to look.

"Reya," said Nina suddenly. She pointed, and I turned to see a tiny door on the other side of the street. Above it was a small sign, hanging below the broken street lamp. "What does it say?" she asked. "I can't read the script—"

I squinted to read the sign. "The Flying Tiger," I read softly.

She gasped, seizing my arm. "The Flying Tiger!"

Our eyes met. "That's what Niam was talking about," Nina hissed. "It's not a *who*—it's a *where!*"

"Keep your voice down," I whispered, but my heart was pounding. We darted across the street and pulled open the door.

The jarring scents of alcohol and curry hit me. I blinked and saw a vast, dingy tavern. The place was windowless, illuminated only by a huge indoor fire pit. The ragged people inside recoiled like insects in the light.

I turned to Nina, and her eyes reflected my disappointment. "It's just a pub," she said. "Why did Niam mention an old bar in his last words?"

I shrugged, trying my best to hide my overwhelming sense of anticlimax. "Let's go inside," I said. "We're getting strange looks just standing here."

We clambered down the wooden steps into the bowels of the bar. Nina found a secluded table in the back. It was so dark that I could only make out the outline of her features, backlit by the fire.

An old barman sidled up to us, eyeing me suspiciously. We each ordered a cup of chai so that he'd leave us alone, and I reluctantly pressed one of our few bronze *rupams* into his palm.

Nina waited until he had limped out of sight before she spoke.

"What do we do?" she said anxiously. "This can't be the right place. I don't even know why Niam led us to this disgusting bar."

She dropped her voice as the old barman returned with the chai, but he heard the last part; he gave her a nasty look, and Nina turned red. We slurped the chai hastily: it didn't taste like anything, but at least it was warm.

"Downtown is crawling with imperial soldiers, so we can't risk going back out there," she continued. The soldier I had seen in the Red Temple flashed in my mind. "And the Renegades have clearly been uptown, because of the painting of your dad, but we have no way of finding them."

Her despair tugged at me. To my annoyance, tears were burning the back of my eyes: tears not for my sake, but for hers. Within six hours, Nina had nearly died, then been forced to witness the massacre of the Renegades. She had spent the past weeks in unrelenting fear. And now, she was trapped in Bharata, suffering because of me once more.

"Nina—" I began, and then I succumbed to the tears.

She reached for my hand, but I tugged it back.

"Nina, this is my fault. First Niam and Aisha, and now you—"

Her face fell. "Reya, not again," she said. "This was my choice. Right now, stranded in Bharata, there is no place I'd rather be. You can't keep blaming yourself."

"You think you're doing the right thing," I interrupted. She opened her mouth to protest, but I wouldn't let her. "But every time your life is on the line, it hurts me. I'd rather die than see you hurt."

Nina closed her eyes. "I'd die for you," she said quietly, and her words hurt me as much as a physical battering. "Not because you're the Bookweaver, but because you're my best friend. Because you are brave and strong and passionate. Because you'd do the same for me," she added.

I let out a fresh gasp of tears.

"Take it back," I choked out. "You cannot be my martyr. My father, the Renegades—I can't take anyone else. I need you to promise me that if the situation arises again—and it will—you'll put your own life first. Please."

Nina started to respond, but then her eyes widened, looking at someone behind me. I felt a soft hand on my back, and I looked up.

"Father?"

There was no mistaking it. The mane of brown hair, the heart-shaped face, the green eyes, the dimples—

The man stepped back, and his resemblance to the Bookweaver seemed to lessen with distance. This man was stockier, broader, somehow deeper and softer at the same time.

He blinked. "I—I'm not your father, but—" He blinked, then froze. His lips silently formed a word of shock.

"Reya?"

Nina stood up behind me. "Who are you?" she demanded, but I was the one who answered. Memories were flashing through my head, bathed in the buttery sepia of childhood: two men sitting at a table, laughing, their drinks sloshing merrily—warm hands lifting me in the air—smiling, gentle—

"Uncle Roshan," I said softly.

Before I could formulate more words, we were embracing. It had been seven years since I'd last seen him, but for a moment, it felt like nothing had changed.

We broke apart, and that's when I noticed that Roshan was older and sadder than when I had last seen him.

Of course, he probably felt the same way about me.

Uncle Roshan sat down beside me at the table. "Reya," he said. "We got word from the other Renegades that you were on the run from Jahan. I can only assume—Amar?" His voice cracked.

I nodded quietly. "He died three weeks ago," I said, and something seemed to break within my uncle's expression.

"I hate that I wasn't there for him," Roshan said. "I hate that I couldn't speak to him. How could I not know where you were? How couldn't I feel it?" He looked agonized, and I pretended not to notice as he grabbed a dingy napkin to wipe his eyes. "Amar needed me, and I wasn't there for him. I wasn't there for *you*."

I shrugged sadly. "I didn't even know you were still alive," I said. "We'd been living in the Raj for so long, I almost forgot I had a family in Bharata. What—what happened to everyone?"

Roshan bowed his head. "You and I are the last Kandharis," he said, and his words sent a shiver of horror down my spine.

Had it really been that long? Already my mother's voice was hazy in my mind, and my lost grandparents and cousins already nameless, faceless—my worst fear was that my father, too, would be forgotten, a legacy turned to ashes, like everything else I had left behind.

My uncle seemed to read my thoughts. "That's why I joined the Renegades in Bharata seven years ago," he said. "We heard that the king sent a squadron after you—how did you make it here?"

I sighed. "It's a very long story, Roshan," I said. "Is this a safe place to talk?"

Roshan nodded. "The *Flying Tiger* has been the

unofficial Renegade headquarters for years," he said. "Here is as safe as anywhere else."

For the better part of an hour, I told the story of the past seven years. Nina supported me, supplying details where memory failed me or where I was too overcome by emotion. Roshan clenched his fists when I told him about the fate of Niam's Renegades.

"Niam was a good man," Roshan said. "The Renegades have suffered a huge loss."

When we finished, however, my uncle's face was quite steady.

"Reya, Nina," he said. "You've both been through a great deal." He smiled fleetingly at me. "I think I can speak for my brother when I say that Amar would have been so proud of you."

I smiled, and his voice grew serious. "But we need to get you safely out of the city before nightfall. Things in Bharata are about to get dangerous, and I can't let you get hurt."

Nina and I looked at each other. "What do you mean?" Nina asked. "What's happening tonight?"

My uncle hesitated, looking torn.

"Roshan?" I pressed.

He sighed, just like my father used to do when he was about to cave.

"Tonight, the Renegades are launching a coup," he told us. "It's been in the works for months. We're going to take back our city, or die trying."

I felt my heart racing. "You're going to take on the imperial army," I said.

It was not a statement; it was a plea for him to tell me I was wrong, that he was not about to risk his life fighting the Zakir dynasty. But Roshan nodded grimly.

"We're severely outnumbered, but it's now or never," he said. "We've waited far too long to let anyone else die."

I knew he was referring to my father when he said that, but I still wasn't convinced.

"It's going to be so dangerous," I said. "I've seen first-hand how ruthless Jahan can be. You could lose everything."

Roshan shrugged. "Maybe," he said. "But we've already lost everything, Reya. At some point, you have to stop lying down and taking it. You have to fight, because your life doesn't mean anything without your dignity."

In that moment, he sounded so much like my father that it hurt.

My voice shook. "If you're fighting, I'm not leaving this city." Next to me, Nina nodded her approval. "I want to stay."

I could see the opposition in my uncle's face, but before he could speak, I pressed on. "I just found you. I'm not losing you again," I said. "There's no way I'm running away while you risk everything."

Roshan sighed. "In that case, I had better introduce you both to the rest of the resistance," he said.

Nina and I smiled at once, and he couldn't help but return it.

Uncle Roshan led us down a set of crooked stone steps in the back of the tavern. "Bharata is the only city that never really bowed down to Jahan," he explained. "I guess you could say the rebellious streak is in our blood."

We followed him through a dimly lit passage.

"After you escaped, Jahan cracked down on us

harder than ever. There are soldiers everywhere and strict rationing is in place, keeping Bharata hungry and cautious. It forced the Renegades to go underground."

He stopped in front of a heavy wooden door. Roshan knocked twice, and it opened. We followed him inside to see a huge table covered in diagrams, notes, and weapons—*war plans.*

Around the table stood almost a dozen Renegades, listening to a woman who was holding a map.

The woman glanced at us. "Roshan," she said. "Don't tell me you've brought more mouths to feed off the Flying Tiger's hospitality."

I looked to my uncle, but Roshan merely laughed. "Not just any mouths," he said. "I brought the most wanted mouths in Kasmira."

The woman finally took a good look at my face, and I saw the map flutter from her hand.

"Reya Kandhari," she said, to nobody in particular. "Now I've seen it all."

An old man at the back of the room looked up excitedly. "She looks just like her father," he said. I felt my cheeks redden as the entire room turned to stare.

"Amar Kandhari," said another Renegade wonderingly. "Where is he?"

"Dead," said Roshan simply. "The king's soldiers killed him a few weeks ago."

For a moment, nobody spoke. I saw the old man lower his head, and grief bit at my stomach.

"This is my niece, Reya Kandhari, and her friend Nina Nadeer," Roshan announced into the shocked silence. "They're here to join the resistance."

The woman seemed to break out of her shock first. She extended an authoritative hand to me. "I'm Kali," she said. "It's an honor, Bookweaver, and I'm sorry for your loss. Have a seat. We have a lot to discuss."

We sat down quickly; I saw Nina gaze in wonder at the maps sprawled before her. Kali resumed her announcements.

"As we've known for a while now, we're severely outnumbered," she said. "At this moment, there are four imperial soldiers for every Renegade, and that number's bound to go up as Jahan sends in reinforcements. His son's already in the city."

Roshan's fist tightened around his sword. "Devendra Zakir is here?"

The memory of the prince, silhouetted atop the mountains, flashed through my mind, and fury surged through me.

Kali nodded gravely. "Unfortunately, yes. The little knuckle-dragger's here, and he's brought his daddy's army. So there's really only one way we can win this thing."

"We spring a trap," said Nina.

Kali glanced at her, surprised. "That's right," she said, approval in her voice; Nina beamed. "We have the home field advantage. If we create a distraction by the fortress uptown, we have enough fighters to steal the reserve cannons hidden in the Red Temple."

Roshan stood up. "We have a major issue," he said. "Reya says that Niam's unit was captured by Prince Devendra's battalion. We were relying on them to spring the trap uptown. Without them, there's no way we can lure enough soldiers out of the fortress."

Kali's face darkened, and I felt a collective anguish in the air. "Then who can draw out the soldiers?" someone asked.

In the silence, my mind was spinning. Maybe there still was a way to lure the imperial soldiers uptown. There was only one person in the entire kingdom who King Jahan would stop at nothing to capture. And that person was—

"Me," I said.

Everyone turned towards me, and I felt myself redden once more. "I can be that distraction," I continued. "I'm the most wanted person in Kasmira. And if I can get out there, I can prove to the people of Bharata that the king hasn't managed to break me yet."

Kali shook her head vehemently. "Do you have any idea how dangerous that is, Reya?" she said. "You'll get yourself killed. There's no way we can guarantee your safety."

"If the plan works, there will be no need for guarantees," I argued. "You'll have seized the city by then, and we'll all be liberated."

I turned to Roshan for support. "You know it's the only way we win this fight."

He sighed. "If your father were alive, he wouldn't—" he started.

"He's not," I cut across sharply.

I didn't mean to say it with a bite, but the words slid off my tongue, razor sharp. "He's dead. Because of Jahan, neither of us will ever know what he would or wouldn't have let me do. So help me avenge him. Please," I added.

I could see the emotions battling on his face: it is impossible to change a person's mind on important things, but some things are so important that you cannot help but try.

"All right," Roshan said at last. He gazed at me with

an expression I could not discern. It took me a moment to recognize it to be pride. "You're a lot more like your father than I remembered."

Ten

If I hadn't known better, I could have walked the entire length of the city and never guessed that a battle was brewing. But the war effort was forming: clandestine, hidden.

As the afternoon wore into evening, Nina and I started to notice Renegades appearing everywhere—leaning against doorways and lining the roofs, virtually invisible under the cover of twilight. In concealed alleys, fighters were building defenses and assembling homemade firepower. Without anyone suspecting, they'd raised an army. They'd sprung a trap.

Roshan briefed us quickly as the sun sank in the sky. My pulse throbbed against my ribcage, and I rubbed my pearl to calm myself.

Within minutes, a plan was pieced together: Nina and I would create enough of a disturbance to lure imperial soldiers out of the fortress. Then we'd lead them deep into the uptown slums, leaving the Renegades free to steal the cannons in the Red Temple.

The plan was incredibly risky. I loved it.

"At sunset, the uptown poor will be gathered for food rationing," Roshan was saying. "The soldiers will be on top guard, because it's no secret that uptown has strong Renegade leanings. You and Nina will need to blend in with the crowd until you see the opportunity to reveal yourselves."

Roshan nodded to me. "Reya, we're counting on you to persuade the citizens of Bharata to stand up tonight, or at least stand aside."

His tone was even enough, but I could sense the urgency beneath it. I understood my duty: as the Bookweaver's daughter, my words could be incredibly influential. Amar Kandhari's legacy had the power to rally a city to fight.

With mere moments remaining until sunset, Nina and I made our way uptown to the fortress. I could tell she was getting nervous: she kept fiddling with Roshan's sword, which was sheathed beneath her cloak.

The rationing took place in the courtyard of the fortress, with stone vaults guarding the barrels of rice and grain. The crowd swelled within roped-off areas, forming an unruly queue that was only barely subdued by the threatening presence of imperial soldiers. The commander himself stood on an elevated platform, watching the crowd with hawkish concentration. I caught a glimpse of his purple eyes, and my heart pounded.

It was Prince Devendra.

"It's almost as if he's expecting us," Nina hissed. Our Renegade escorts, positioned discreetly near the fortress, had also noticed the crown prince: I saw them whispering nervously among themselves.

"It doesn't matter," I muttered. "We can't back down. Now's our only shot to take back the city."

She sighed. "You're right. At least we'll get some revenge on him for all the hell he's put us through."

That hadn't occurred to me. Despite myself, I grinned.

Just then, Prince Devendra lifted a huge gong and struck it with his sword. The noise reverberated painfully through the crowd, silencing us.

"Citizens of Bharata," he announced. "You are gathered tonight to benefit from his Majesty's generosity in receiving rations for your labor."

Even from thirty feet away—too far to see the fury in his eerie purple eyes—Devendra had a way with crowds. His very presence was menacing, despite the fact that he was no older than sixteen—perhaps the cruelty was just in his blood. The crowd began to murmur discontentedly, but they were silenced with another gong.

"But let it be known," Devendra said, more loudly this time, "that his Majesty does not tolerate dissent. It has not escaped my father's notice that uptown Bharata's loyalty to the Zakir dynasty has always been ... shaky."

The crowd shifted uncomfortably, and I remembered what Roshan said about uptown being full of Renegade sympathizers. But from the way people were whispering, it was clear that this proclamation was out of the ordinary.

"Therefore, King Jahan wishes to provide the citizens of Bharata with another chance to prove their loyalty," he continued. "As you know, my regiment has been tracking a special fugitive through Kasmira." Devendra spread his arms, and on cue, hundreds of banners unfurled from the fortress, creating a palpable breeze.

My heart caught in my throat at the sight of my own

portrait, hundreds of which glared blankly back at me.

"Damn it," Nina whispered in miserable awe as her wanted poster unfurled beside mine. I shrunk back, unable to shake the claustrophobic sense that the crowd was suffocating us. All it took was one person to turn around and recognize us—

"Reya Kandhari, aged fifteen. Nina Nadeer, aged sixteen," said Devendra. He held up the wanted poster. "Any Bharata citizen who has information about—"

The next moments happened so fast, I barely had time to process.

An arrow whizzed out of nowhere, piercing the wanted poster in Devendra's hand. The crowd bellowed as Roshan's second arrow rained down, hitting the prince in the shoulder, and Devendra tumbled off the platform and out of sight—

Before I could register what had just happened, Nina had seized my hand, and we were tearing through the shocked crowd. I climbed onto the platform where Devendra had stood just seconds ago, because now was my only chance to finish my father's fight.

It was pandemonium. Soldiers rushed forward to stop me, but Renegades materialized out of nowhere and engaged them in combat. The peasants below were stunned, frozen like statues.

Someone looked up at me. The cry of recognition spread like wildfire, and within a minute, the entire fortress had realized that Reya Kandhari, the most wanted person in Kasmira, was standing on the platform before them.

A little wildly, Nina seized the gong and banged it. It worked like magic: for a second time, the crowd went silent.

I glanced at Nina desperately, my tongue turning to lead. I couldn't do this. I couldn't form the words to rally the crowd to listen to me, let alone take up arms.

"People—people of Bharata," I began. My voice didn't sound like my own.

I took a deep breath, my eyes traveling across the crowd, landing on random strangers: a teenage girl who looked no older than Nina. A dark-skinned man who could have easily been my own father. An old woman clutching her daughter to her chest. And all at once, I realized what I hadn't before.

I didn't need to be afraid of them. They were people just like me.

"My name is Reya Kandhari," I said. "I'm the Bookweaver's daughter, and we all have a lot in common."

Nina smiled, steadying me. I pushed on.

"Over the last seven years, we've all suffered in silence. We've all had our legacies stolen. We've all lost someone we loved. And we've all been made to feel worthless by Jahan Zakir."

The crowd was silent. The battle shouts before me seemed to deaden. I felt the same glowing warmth that I had only felt twice before: the pulsing rhythm of belonging, the rush of power and possibility that simply felt like *magic.*

"I know you're like me," I continued. "Not just because you've suffered, but because you refuse to back down. Because you're too strong to give up. Because you, like me, believe that together, we are more powerful than any tyrant and his teenage son."

From within the crowd, someone let out a whoop of affirmation. I raised my hand, and the crowd quieted again. My heart was thumping.

"My father once told me that we always have a choice to make: between sitting back or fighting. Between being scared or being kind. Between barely surviving or actually living."

I paused.

"So today, we have a choice to make. We have to choose between letting King Jahan hold us down, or telling him that we sure as hell aren't going to take it anymore."

Beside me, Nina tugged my arm urgently: we were running out of time. But I wasn't finished. I took one last deep breath.

"I know what choice I'm going to make tonight," I said. "The question is, do you?"

Someone shouted in agreement. The cries multiplied, and before I could comprehend what was happening, the people around me were chanting in support. I saw weapons appear in the crowd: clubs, sticks, and even empty pans—Bharata had made its choice. The city was cheering, literally in the face of danger.

That's when the fortress of Bharata exploded.

I whirled around to see the massive wall behind me collapse like a deck of tarot cards. Then the blast impact hit and I was catapulting back into Nina, who barely managed to catch me. The wanted posters on the walls burst into flames, and dust billowed everywhere.

The imperial army had arrived.

As one, the peasants below rushed to engage the soldiers, even as the earth erupted beneath their feet, sending thick clouds of rock spiraling like towers into the sky. Nina and I staggered back as arrows—whether friendly or not, I couldn't tell—rained down on us.

"The Renegades can hold them off," gasped Nina,

ducking as an entire table sailed over her head. "We need to get out of here—"

Out of the corner of my eye, I caught a flicker of movement, and with a jolt of horror I saw Prince Devendra clamber back onto of the platform beside us, very much alive, the arrow still lodged in his shoulder. He raised his sword, and my stomach jumped into my throat.

"Nina, *look out!*"

My body went into autopilot as I tackled Nina out of the way—the blade missed us by a hair. Then Devendra was standing over me and I was scuttling back desperately. His grin was unnerving as he lifted his sword for a second swing—

"No!"

Nina appeared out of nowhere, and I rolled away just in time. She smashed the gong into Devendra's head, an almost inhuman expression on her face—I knew she was thinking of revenge. With a strangely muffled clang, Devendra crumpled over the platform's edge and disappeared once more.

"Nina, that was the most awesome thing I've ever seen—"

She grinned at me, but stopped short as a flaming lamp rolled across the stage, narrowly missing our feet. The flour bags caught on fire—

I seized her hand and we leapt behind the platform, narrowly missing Devendra's prone form. Together, we tore through the now-empty ration queue, the fight raging around us. A hand seized at my cloak, and I turned to see a single imperial soldier who had somehow broken through the peasant ranks—

For a moment, I was dragged back by his sheer strength, and I felt my hand slip from Nina's—then the

soldier went limp, and my mind pieced together a series
of images: the arrow sprouting from his arm, a lone
archer standing on the wall of the ruined fortress, pulling
back his hood. Roshan, his hand still on his bow, nodded
briefly to me before Nina tugged me away again—

We ran from the burning fortress like we had never
run before. We ran because we were scared out of our
wits and had no idea how else to survive such a mad-
ness. We ran because for the first time, we were aware
of just how many lives depended on it.

Nina and I tore downtown, passing by pockets of
violent fighting. Skirmishes had broken out all over the
streets between Renegades and imperial soldiers.
Entire buildings fell like toys, Zakir banners blazing
from the roofs.

"Halt!"

I turned so fast I almost slipped.

Thundering down the street behind us were nearly
a dozen soldiers. They had already seen us: there was
no time to hide. Nina seized an abandoned peddler's
cart and flung it at them with a strength I didn't know
she had—two were knocked over, but the rest dodged
and kept coming.

"This way, Reya—"

I followed Nina around the corner of the street.
"Here!" I said. We dashed through a jasmine-curtained
archway. In an awful moment, I realized that we were
not on another street, but in the yard of someone's
bungalow. We had trapped ourselves.

The soldiers burst into the courtyard, shredding the
jasmine to pieces. Before they could regroup, we had
thrown open the doors and tumbled into the bungalow. Nina's fingers flew to latch the door behind us.

The walls immediately began to creak. The soldiers were trying to smash the door open.

Nina was knocking over bookcases, tandoori stoves, statues—anything to slow them down as we searched for an exit. We dashed into the kitchen just as the soldiers broke down the door and chased us deep into the house. Nina and I backtracked desperately, but it was too late.

"Put down the sword, Nadeer," one of them said. "You've put up a good fight, but it's time to surrender."

The soldiers fanned out in the kitchen, pulling out their swords, almost lazily. They had us cornered. I could see Nina hesitate, her eyes darting for an escape.

I tried to buy her time, even though my gut told me it was futile. "We're never going t—"

Nina yelped and shoved me out of harm's way as the soldier collapsed without warning. His sword flew out of his grip and impaled the floor between our feet.

Standing behind him was a monster of a man, his face hooded as he slashed at the remaining soldiers. They cowered under the onslaught, superior in number but helpless against the element of surprise—

Our savior pulled off his hood, and my heart leapt in a tumultuous rush of emotions.

"Niam!"

I ran to Niam and threw my arms around him, which hurt—he was wearing armor beneath his clothes.

"How are you here?" gasped Nina. "We thought you were—"

"Dead?" interrupted Niam. He grinned. "Nina, they'd have a hard time keeping my ghost out of a brawl like this."

She laughed, the relief evident in her voice. "How did you get away?"

His face was grave as he answered, searching the fallen soldiers for weapons. "Devendra was a little distracted with the siege of Bharata. He took his best soldiers with him, so I managed to overpower my guards en route to the Raj. But Aisha, Aran, the others … they were taken to the *mahal.*"

Niam stood up and handed me a sword. It felt like a tree trunk in my arms, heavy and unbalanced.

"You're going to need this," he told me. "It's getting worse out there. Roshan's covering us from the roof, but we need to get someplace safe."

I hefted the sword with both hands; it felt alien and unwelcome. Niam noticed my discomfort.

"You'll get the hang of it," he told me, the faintest trace of humor in his voice, despite everything. "If a soldier comes at you, just stick it in them. Not much to it, really."

Nina nodded reassuringly at me, and we headed outside. The street was mercifully clear, but I could hear the sounds of battle just blocks away.

"Reya!"

My uncle climbed down from the rooftop, cat-like in his agility. He had a nasty cut across his shoulder, but he looked otherwise uninjured. "It's getting too dangerous out here. You and Nina need to wait in the Flying Tiger."

There was no time to debate the point. He and Niam exchanged terse nods of understanding. With that, the four of us began to run, the battle searing through the city.

As the sun sank and the shadows thickened, the Renegades were backed up yard by yard until we were nearly a league from the city's center in any direction.

Sometimes it was Nina at my side, slashing enemies with her sword like she'd been doing it all her life. Other times, it was Niam pulling me forward, Roshan's arrows whistling through the blur of tangled smoke. The fights raged as we headed downtown towards the Red Temple, but I knew it wasn't going to be enough.

Niam led us through a side alley. There was a gap in the street where a building had collapsed, and for the first time, I saw Bharata cracking under pressure.

I had seen losing fights before, but nothing like the battle before me.

The Renegades were trying to seize the Red Temple's cannons, but the imperial soldiers were putting up a spirited fight. Even more of them were returning from the fortress, which could only mean one thing: uptown had fallen to the soldiers.

Everything seemed to slow down as another explosion rocked the Red Temple, sending flames arcing down the street. My senses deadened, as though I was hearing it all through a thick curtain.

I didn't need to see any of the destruction. I just needed to look at my uncle's eyes to know that it was all over.

Next to me, Nina groaned, and my senses started working at once: I heard the collective wail of a defeated army as the Renegades were swamped, saw the fire engulf the sky, and felt the smoke pool deep within my lungs.

Roshan looked back at me urgently. "You both shouldn't be here," he said.

I hesitated, and he touched my shoulder softly. "You were brave tonight," he said. "I'm sorry."

I opened my mouth, but no words occurred to me. We had gambled an entire city, and we had lost. What was left to say?

He nodded sadly at me, like he understood exactly how I felt. Then he and Niam turned and rushed into the fray.

The Flying Tiger was empty when Nina and I returned. Even the old barman was gone; I wondered briefly whether he was still alive. The tables were cleared, chairs stacked neatly in rows, as though the bar had finally closed for business.

I followed Nina down the darkened steps into the basement. She found a lantern and lit it, engulfing the small room in light. The stone walls of the Flying Tiger muffled the noise from the street fights, which I was grateful for.

At last, Nina spoke. "So what do we do now?"

I was silent for a moment. "I don't know. Hopefully Roshan will be back soon."

I didn't want to make a plan, not now, not anymore. I didn't want to be responsible for my own survival. For once, I wanted someone else to take care of me, to tell me what to do.

"Do you—do you think there's any way we can leave Bharata now?"

I took a deep breath, the fear swelling like billowing silk. "How do you expect me to know that, Nina?"

She didn't say anything else after that. Although I felt bad for snapping, I was relieved that I no longer had to answer her. Because I didn't need any more reminders that tonight's disaster was all my fault.

My thoughts were interrupted by the sounds of several gongs, struck in unison.

Nina and I glanced at each other. Without another word, we tore up the steps and into the bar. She stood behind me as I lifted a corner of the window curtain to look outside.

Standing along every street corner was a soldier with a gong, creating a message system that criss-crossed the city. As one, the soldiers rung the gongs again and recited a message, their voices echoing in unison through the deserted street.

"His Majesty, King Jahan, applauds the bravery of Bharata," they said. Their uniform precision was truly eerie. "However, your time has come. Already, you have lost nearly a thousand men and surrendered the cannons and the fortress. Your defeat will be soon, and it will be swift."

Next to me, Nina pressed her ear to the glass, trying to listen better.

"But there is no need for that, because his Majesty is not without mercy. He wishes to offer Bharata a trade: one life in exchange for thousands spared."

I didn't dare look at Nina, too terrified of missing a word—

"Bring Reya Kandhari or Nina Nadeer to the Red Temple clock tower, and the bloodshed will end."

Then—"You have until midnight."

The soldiers rang their gongs again and filed away. I shrank back from the window, heart pounding. Behind me, I could hear Nina's rapid breathing. "Nina—"

"Don't even think about it," snarled Nina. There was something behind her expression that I couldn't discern, but it gutted me—for the first time, I was seeing her panic.

I hesitated, and she seized my arm. "Take one more step towards the door, and I swear I'll—"

She practically dragged me down the basement stairs, slamming the door and flinging me into a chair.

I tried again. "Nina," I said. "Shouldn't we at least discuss this?"

She looked angrier than I'd ever seen her. "What's there to say that hasn't already been said twenty times over?" she demanded. "You are not turning yourself in. That's final."

I was the one who was angry now. I understood, then, what my father meant when he said that anger only came from fear or love: I couldn't let Nina go, and she couldn't let go of me.

"Damn it, Nina!" I snapped. "How am I supposed to let thousands of innocent people die because I didn't turn myself in? How many people is my life worth?"

Despite myself, I glanced at the clock—less than two hours until midnight. We were running out of time.

I whirled on her. "And *you!* You cannot turn yourself in, either. You've already lost so much because of me."

"Don't flatter yourself," said Nina coldly. "You don't hold a monopoly on all of the pain in my life that has led me to this point."

Her voice was furious, but I was glad that Nina was fighting back—at least her anger provided a small, although misguided, outlet for my guilt.

She seemed to sense this, because when Nina next spoke, her voice was gentle. "But this isn't about me. You're a hero, Reya. You're a symbol to so many people. If you give up now, the Renegades—and *your father*—died for nothing."

Blood pounded in my ears.

"I'M NOT WORTH DYING FOR!" I screamed, and before I could control it, the magic surged through my nerves for the second time in my life.

The table before me cracked in half.

Nina gasped as splinters flew everywhere—one grazed her cheek, leaving a shallow cut. The sight of her blood sent spasms of terror down my spine, and I felt the magic recede.

"Oh my god, Nina, I'm so sorry—"

She staggered back, and all I could see was the horror on her face. It hit me in that terrifying, towering moment— I had hurt my best friend. She was afraid of me.

Nina disguised her reaction, but the damage was done. Guilt made me feel as though my heart was being poked with a cold rod, and I fell back into the chair.

"It's okay, Reya." Nina's voice was warm and sooth- ing, shaping words which were meant to heal me, but hurt me anyways. "You don't have to be the one who dies. Let's make a deal."

I looked at her through my tears. Nina continued. "I will not turn myself in if you swear that you won't, either."

She waited for my response, but I could only man- age a weak nod. My mind was already planning for what would have to happen tonight.

Nina was tearing up a little too, now. "Reya. I need you to promise."

Somehow, I managed to find a smile and plaster it on my face. "I promise, Nina," I said.

She stared deep into my eyes as if looking for deceit, but she couldn't find any—I was made of stone, and stone doesn't feel.

All I could see was her wounded cheek. She touched

my shoulder gently, as if she couldn't feel her injury. I
knew she was pretending.

Nina blew out the lamps, and there was nothing
but silence until both of us were asleep. I knew what
I had to do.

Eleven

My eyes adjusted to the darkness when I awoke an hour later. Nina's sleeping form was a dark shadow near the window. I climbed the stairs without creaking, slipping my father's pearl into my pocket for safekeeping. And then I walked away from my best friend.

"I'd die for you," Nina had told me at the tavern. And in that moment, I knew what I had to do. Because when you care about someone, you're a goner. You put their life before yours, no matter how painful it feels—even if it means giving up your own.

My heart rattled as I hurried past the shuttered windows; the faintest cracks of light shone through the hastily boarded doors. It felt like I was racing against the clock—not just against the clock tower which ticked towards midnight, but against the unstoppable passage of time that had pushed me towards defeat for the past seven years.

Still, it hurt. I was terrified of a world that moved on without me. Did it make me pathetic, selfish, to wish that the world would stop when I did? Would my father be proud of me for dying, or would he be ashamed? I didn't know. I still don't.

I could see it now: the Red Temple, dwarfed beneath the enormous clock tower. Standing at the Temple was a group of imperial soldiers. I shrank into the shadows, glancing up at the clock face—five minutes until midnight. It wasn't too late to turn back.

Behind me, someone gasped, and I whirled around into the darkness.

I heard a match strike—then a lantern bloomed to life, and I was staring into a pair of familiar gray eyes.

"*Nina?*"

She shifted the lantern to illuminate her face, and my heart sunk.

"Reya," she said. "You were going to turn yourself in?"

"Nina," I said, and my voice cracked. "You need to go back, where it's safe." I could tell her hands were shaking from the way the light bobbed, casting shadows around the alley.

"And let you go and turn yourself into those soldiers? No way."

I might have laughed at the irony. After all we had been through, Nina was going to be the one who prevented me from saving her life.

"Come on, Nina," I murmured. "You and I both know that this is the only way it can end. It's always been the only way."

Her eyes filled with tears. "No," she whispered, almost childishly. "You don't have to do this."

"Wait a minute," I hissed. "What are *you* doing here, Nina?"

Nina looked down, and the betrayal felt like a dull punch to my gut. "You were going to turn yourself in," I said. "After we specifically agreed that you needed to stay safe."

Her face fell. "You're the Bookweaver, for God's sake," she said. "This is a sacrifice I'm willing to make. Not just because you're a Yogi, but because you're my best friend."

There was no time to argue, not when five minutes remained before the city of Bharata went down in flames. Each beat of my heart was a tick of the clock, but in that moment, my breath was steady.

I turned and ran towards the Red Temple. I heard her anguished cry behind me as I collided with a soldier who seemed to materialize out of nowhere.

It all happened so fast—I was seized by the arm, and before I could stop her, Nina rushed into the Temple to protect me. My stupid, compassionate, courageous best friend tried to save me from a dozen armed soldiers, tried to save me from my martyr aspirations. She couldn't.

We were overpowered in seconds and thrown to the ground. Nina was dragged one way, and I was dragged another. I saw her dark head disappear into the back of a carriage, and that was the last thing I saw before something long and slender—a needle— appeared in the periphery of my vision, piercing my neck, and everything flickered—

Despite everything, I kept thinking about something my father told me in his final days. He said that sometimes what we think was meant for us doesn't exist. We may bleed for it, we may sweat for it, and we may even sacrifice ourselves for it, but what we search for cannot always be ours.

When I opened my eyes, everything was bright. Was this what the afterlife looked like?

I blinked rapidly and watched the world come into focus.

I was sitting inside what appeared to be a ship—I could tell from the rhythmic swaying of the waters below. Through the small window, enclosed by bars, early daylight streamed.

"Nina?" I shouted.

"You awake, witch?"

I turned in alarm to see two helmeted soldiers standing in the brig before me, blocking the exit. I tried to get up but realized I couldn't—my hands were strapped to the arms of my seat. Panic hit me in a dizzying wave.

"I—what's going on? Where are we going?"

One soldier pulled off his helmet, and my stomach tightened in hatred. It was Prince Devendra.

He looked well, considering the fact that he'd been gonged in the face and left for dead.

"That doesn't concern you," he said.

He and his fellow soldier stepped in front of me. In spite of my situation, I felt smug satisfaction at the sight of the bandages across Devendra's forehead.

Devendra paced back and forth musingly.

"For the most wanted person in Kasmira, you're not particularly powerful," he said. "Here I was chasing you across the kingdom, preparing myself to fight a hardened Mage, someone worthy of being the Bookweaver's daughter. But you have no idea what you're doing, do you?"

"I could say the same about you," I said, before I could stop myself. "I hope you'll invest in better armor, now that Nina and I have beaten you up on two separate occasions."

He smirked. "You're nothing but bluster," he said. "But you're my ticket back into my father's good graces, so I'm not complaining. Let's get started."

The crown prince pulled off his cloak and threw it on the ground, revealing scarred, muscled arms.

"You're in so much trouble with his Majesty. You're under arrest for treason, inciting rebellions, illegal magic—the list goes on. So if you want to survive this, I'd suggest you start talking to us."

Devendra pulled up a chair, but I wasn't paying attention. My mind was racing.

Why was I still breathing? Devendra had certainly gotten the chance to kill me back at the Red Temple. There was only one explanation: he was taking me back to the Raj. The king wanted me alive.

"As imperial commander and heir to the Zakir throne," said Devendra, interrupting my thoughts, "most traitors don't get the honor of being interrogated by me. You should count yourself incredibly lucky—or unlucky."

"Please," I said. "You're just a kid with daddy issues."

He flinched, but the shadow over his face passed quickly. "I could say the same about you," he said. He shook his hair out of his eyes, all haughtiness returned. "Tell me, how did it feel when I blew up half your pathetic friends? What'd they call themselves—the Renegades?"

He laughed—terribly, easily.

I raised my eyebrows and leaned back in my chair, successfully hiding my fury.

"Where's Nina?" I asked.

Devendra shrugged. "That doesn't concern you," he said. "If you're sitting on a chair before me, you should be a lot more worried about yourself."

He was already studying my reaction in measured, sweeping glances.

Two could play at his game. I felt my cold mental wall of defense go up.

I smiled. "Your concern is appreciated," I said. "Now, if you don't mind, can we get on with it?"

Devendra smiled back. If it wasn't for the cruelty in his eyes, he was almost handsome.

"I have a feeling you're the key to it all," he said. "What makes you so special, Kandhari, that the city of Bharata, which has remained uneasy but silent for seven years, risked everything for you?"

I sunk back into my chair. "Believe me, I'm still asking myself that. Next question."

The other soldier opened his mouth indignantly, but Devendra silenced him with a hand. "Fair enough. Who was the leader of the rebellion?"

"Where is Nina?" I repeated. "I know that you have her, Zakir. Tell me, how did it feel when she smashed your pretentious little face into next week?"

Devendra's eyebrows raised slightly, but he didn't react. "I'm not going to tell you anything," he said.

I smirked. "Neither am I."

Now the prince was getting riled, and my inner fighter cheered, but only for an instant, because Devendra had a new question. "Have it your way,

Kandhari. In that case, what do you know about the Renegades?"

His eyes met mine, and I felt his purple-ringed pupils swallow me whole. I was screwed, and I knew it. How long could I survive an imperial interrogation? And where was King Jahan?

"Clearly, more than you know about basic economics," I said. "Because the way I understand it, two parties can't make a trade unless they both have something to offer. So unless you're going to tell me where Nina is, I know nothing about the Renegades."

For the first time, Devendra looked truly angry. He stood up, knocking his chair over with a clatter. At his full height, he towered over me. "You stupid little—"

His voice was drowned out by an ear-splitting lurch as our ship ground to a halt. The impact sent my chair skidding; Devendra himself nearly lost his balance. He jerked up angrily. "What the—"

On the deck above us, the cabin door burst open and someone descended the wooden steps. A pair of legs appeared first, then arms draped in black satin, until the entire woman came into view.

She pulled back her veil and revealed her face. It was cold and solemn, her pallid skin thrown in unflattering contrast by her dark robes. In a horrible moment, I recognized her to be Lady Sharati, the veiled Mage who had nearly captured me at the river. She turned to glance at me, and her golden cat's eyes met mine.

Devendra looked, if possible, even angrier. "What is the meaning of this, Lady Sharati?" he demanded. "You have no right to barge into my ship and interrupt my interrogation after I dismissed you—"

"I don't answer to dishonored princes. I'm here on

orders of King Jahan," Sharati interrupted smugly. "There's been a change in plans. His Majesty now wants the Bookweaver released into my custody. So if you'll untie her—"

Devendra planted himself firmly in front of me, glaring at Sharati.

"No way. You're not taking her. *I* laid siege to the entire city of Bharata to capture this girl for my father."

Sharati smirked. "I'm sure you'll have time to tell him all about your conquests if he *ever* invites you onto the Council," she said with delicate stress. "In the meantime, I'd be glad to pass on a message."

The soldier beside him fidgeted nervously. Devendra blushed purple, which clashed oddly with his eye color. He looked more rattled than ever.

"Fine, then. Take her. Good luck getting anything out of her."

"We'll see," said Lady Sharati. She pointed a finger at me, and I felt the straps on my wrists split apart with a sizzle.

"Come with me, Bookweaver," she ordered. I stood up, rubbing my wrists, too stunned at what she had just done to disobey.

I followed Sharati up the stairs, taking care to glare at Devendra as we crossed the gangplank. We stepped off the ship onto a deserted dockyard, my legs shaking slightly from hours of disuse. Devendra's battleship, now emptied of its precious cargo, bobbed dismally on the oil-black river.

"Welcome to the royal grounds, Bookweaver," said the Mage in clipped tones. "I am Lady Sharati, his Majesty's personal Mage. The king will receive you shortly. He has placed you in my care, and you will present yourself to his Council today. First, I will be taking you to your quarters."

I blinked. "My quarters?"

Sharati frowned at me, like I was being daft on purpose. "Your quarters," she repeated. "You will be living in the *mahal* as Jahan Zakir's personal guest."

I stumbled to keep up with her long strides. "I thought he wanted to kill me."

Sharati's face was impassive. "Like I said, change in plans."

I was silent for a moment, struggling to keep up with the new turn of events.

"Where's Nina?" I asked at last.

The woman finally stopped striding and turned to face me. Her cat's eyes latched on mine.

"Lady Kandhari, I am only going to say this once," she said. "From this moment onwards, Nina Nadeer is dead to you. If you mention that peasant's name, or disobey the king in any way, I shall see to it that she becomes dead in a very literal sense."

I felt as though she had stabbed me.

Nina was going to be used against me. She had become everything I feared: a pawn in this game, bait to draw me in, collateral damage.

I took a deep breath to control my emotions, but my pulse rocketed again as we rounded the crest in the hill.

Standing before me was the *mahal* itself. Somehow, it was even more magnificent in person—far grander than the dark paper cutout I had gazed at from my mango tree for the past seven years. It was solid and sprawling, dominated by teardrop-shaped domes, barbed minarets spiraling into the misty sky.

A squadron of royal guards saluted us smartly as we passed through a pair of massive gates. They followed me like an entourage into the *mahal.*

It was like nothing I had ever seen before. Arches guarded by stoic stone tigers. Broad columns. Carved wood and polished stone, a maze vast and deep. Colored glass windows sent light splintering across the floor, suffusing us in colors. Everywhere I looked was the massive *Z,* declaring the Zakirs' indomitable presence.

As Lady Sharati led us down a sunlit corridor, the servants and guards bustling around stopped to stare at me—some with awe, some with open hostility. I ignored them, focusing instead on the train of Sharati's veil.

The guards ushered me through a doorway, surrounding me like a human prison. I stepped inside to behold a bed of satin pillows, lined by shelves of books and endless furniture. There were even mirrors, a luxury I'd never had access to in the Fringes. The enormous window overlooked the hills, dwarfing the entire Raj.

Sharati hustled me inside, glancing at the clock. "These are your chambers," she said. "You will eat, sleep, and study here every night."

She pointed to a small bell hanging by the door. "His Majesty has arranged for servants to attend to your every need, so that you should never desire to leave. You will ring this bell to summon them."

I swore silently to myself that I would never use it.

Lady Sharati had scarcely rung the bell when my servants filed in: three girls who were hardly older than me, silent and meek. "Hello," I told them.

One of the servants gasped.

Sharati made a noise of displeasure. "Lady Kandhari, you will never address your servants like that," she snapped. "They are not your equals. They may not speak to you unless responding to a direct order."

The girls wouldn't meet my eyes. I ignored the pinch at my throat. Did they have any idea that just a month ago, I had been one of them: poor, disrespected, terrified to look anyone with power in the eye?

"She's due to the Council in half an hour. You three will bathe her," Sharati ordered the servants, who jumped a little before leading me to the bathroom. Like everything in the palace, it was magnificent, centered around a gilded bath of steaming water.

As I peeled off my shirt, I glanced at my reflection in the surface of the glistening bath. To my shock, I saw my servants reflected in the water, still standing expectantly behind me.

I whirled around, hastily pulling my shirt back on. "Do you mind giving me a moment?"

The braver girl looked fleetingly up at me. "Our orders were to bathe you, miss." She looked quickly back down.

"I can bathe myself," I said. "And you don't have to call me 'miss.'"

The servants exchanged glances, clearly unprepared for such resistance. "But royalty can't be made to bathe themselves," one whispered.

I raised my eyebrows. "I think I can handle it," I said.

"Our orders were to—"

My chest knotted. "Fine. Fine. Bathe me, follow your orders. I don't care."

The girls looked relieved, and despite the situation, a mixture of guilt and pity bit at me. I ignored my embarrassment as they helped me out of my clothes, their hands hesitant and cautious.

"What are your names?" I asked the girls as they helped me into the bath. They hesitated, and I added, "That's an order."

"Kira Chadav," whispered the bright-haired one, with the hint of a smile that I couldn't help but return. "And these are Trisha Jain and Sita Singh, miss."

"I'm Reya," I said. "You don't have to call me 'miss.'"

The water stung my scrapes as I scrubbed properly for the first time in a month. By the time I stepped out of the bath, the water was several shades darker.

"His Majesty has picked out a dress for you, miss," said Kira. She caught herself. "I mean—he's picked a dress for you, Reya."

She crossed the room and opened the wardrobe.

For a moment, I forgot where I was, because framed in its wooden doors was the most beautiful *sari* I'd ever seen. Tiny silver flowers were sprinkled on green silk like a glimpse of stars in the jungle, flowing into solid midnight. It would have cost a peasant a year's worth of wages.

My servants wrapped it almost reverently around me. With deft fingers, they wove and bobbed around me, brushing out my hair, pinching color into my cheeks. Then Sita turned me around to face the mirror.

The girl in the mirror was elegant in her *sari*, too bright to look at for long. She looked like money, power, and security. I couldn't recognize her staring back at me.

"The color really brings out your eyes, Reya," said Kira quietly. I was too preoccupied to notice that she had finally stopped calling me "miss."

Sita reached for the pearl on my neck, and I jerked my hand up to stop her. She looked confused. "Miss, it's cracked," she started, but I cut her off. "I don't care," I said. "It stays."

"Let her keep it," Kira told her, and Sita shrank back.

There was a sharp knock on the door, and Lady Sharati stepped into the room, wearing a fresh black *sari*, her silk veil over her face. "Come with me, Lady Kandhari. We're behind schedule."

I caught a glimpse of Kira smiling encouragingly before Sharati slammed the door behind us.

Sharati's brisk pace didn't slow as she led me through the winding halls. I stumbled on my skirt when she came to an abrupt halt before a set of huge wooden doors. "His Majesty and the Council await you," she said. "Prepare yourself."

"But what do they want from me?"

"That is the king's prerogative to inform you."

Sharati said it as though the matter was closed for discussion. "You are presenting yourself to his Council now, and you will obey them. I don't have to remind you what happens if you don't."

Nina.

To calm my nerves, I studied the ornate oak doors of the Council—the last barrier between me and the lair of a beast. They were carved with what initially looked like flowers, but actually turned out to be human faces, contorted and twisted in agony. I felt my stomach wringing itself—the faces belonged to Mages, paying the regime's ultimate price.

Lady Sharati nodded, and the doors opened.

Twelve

I walked through the doors with Nina's name still burning on my lips.

The Council was an enormous circular room, and its mirrored walls made it seem dizzyingly larger. Built into the walls were pews that were filled with nobles, reflected thousands of times in the mirrors. They were all staring down at me like I was a beetle in a jar.

My footsteps echoed as I walked into the center of the room.

The floor was inlaid with chips of mirror that sparkled like candles, forming an elaborate mosaic. I suspected I'd have to stand on top of the room to see the whole design properly, but what I saw was staggering enough—stars of ice and fire, surrounding an enormous *Z*.

The room's beauty, however, couldn't disguise the fact that something was obviously missing. The throne in the center of the room was empty. The king hadn't shown.

"Where's my father?"

Devendra Zakir was framed in the Council doors. He was still wearing his military cloak, but he'd pinned on all of his medals. They glinted impressively in the reflected light.

"I was told he'd be here at the Council," he said. "I have an update on the Renegades."

"Awfully brave of you to interrupt us," one of the nobles said, glaring at Devendra. "After what happened in Bharata last night, you're lucky you still bear the Zakir name."

I saw Devendra blanch. "Watch yourself, Lord Raksha," he said, his voice dangerously low; it was only because I knew him so well that I noticed the tremor in his voice. "I'm still the imperial commander of Kasmira. I do not tolerate disrespect."

Lord Raksha looked down at him, his eyes steely. "That remains to be seen," he replied coldly. "His Majesty says that he will deal with you later. At the present, you are barred from this Council."

I savored the outraged look on Devendra's face, but it passed quickly, as Lord Raksha then turned on me.

"Identify yourself," he said.

"My name is Reya Kandhari." I was surprised by how steady my voice sounded. "I'm fifteen years old. I'm the Bookweaver's daughter—"

"This is the Bookweaver?" Lord Raksha wasn't looking at me: he was frowning at Devendra with an air of puzzlement.

"I'm Reya Kandhari," I said again. "I'm—"

"No, no, I get that," Raksha interrupted again. "But you're just a little girl."

Torture, insults, death threats, I could handle. *Little*

girl, not so much.

"Well spotted," I snapped, before I could stop myself.

There was a ripple of gasps, and Lord Raksha's eyes narrowed. He leaned over the front of his pew, robes billowing.

"You'd better learn some respect, Bookweaver's daughter," he said. "You'll need it for the task his Majesty has in mind for you."

"A task?" I echoed, but Raksha interrupted me for the third time.

"He has asked me to assess your skills," he said. "So I ask you, Lady Kandhari, what sort of black arts can you perform?"

"I'm sorry. *Black arts?*"

"Magic," breathed Lord Raksha. He said it reluctantly, like the word was contagious. "Sorcery. Witchcraft. Whatever you call it, his Majesty requires it of you."

I frowned. "I thought the king outlawed magic."

The lords murmured amongst themselves at that.

"Magic is an abomination," admitted Raksha. "As a result, King Jahan only keeps a few loyal Mages in his employ to ward off enemies, and even they must remain veiled in his presence."

He glanced at Lady Sharati. She inclined her chin haughtily beneath her satin veil, and I remembered how Devendra had once called her a freak.

"However, the events in Bharata have caused him to reconsider," Raksha continued. "He recognizes that magic is necessary to fight an even larger evil—the wretched Renegades and other dissidents. Without Mages and Yogis to help enforce the peace, those scoundrels will plague Kasmira and plunge our kingdom into hell."

His words hung in the air, and it took me a moment to find my voice.

"Even if I wanted to," I said, "How could I help Jahan?"

"You're the Bookweaver," said Raksha. "As a result, you possess *vayati,* the black art of making your words come to life."

And at last, I understood.

I understood exactly why the king wanted me alive. It was as though my entire life was a series of falling dominoes, culminating in the horrible realization that threatened to knock me down at last. I finally understood what Jahan wanted me to do.

"You will perform *vayati* for him," said Lord Raksha, confirming my suspicions. "In light of Bharata's rebellion, the king wants you to weave a story that will crush all rebellion and destroy the Mages, solidifying his control over Kasmira."

I could feel the resistance building in me, filling my throat, lungs, and stomach, expanding until I thought I would burst. Because I couldn't do it. I couldn't join King Jahan, help his twisted cause after everything he'd taken from me—

Lord Raksha seemed to read my mind.

"I hope you're not considering resistance, Lady Kandhari," he said, his voice low. "His Majesty has no shortage of ways to convince you otherwise."

The defiance wouldn't leave. It had turned solid, pressing against the cracked pearl I wore on my throat.

"About that," I said. "Slight problem—I never learned to use or control my magic. Let alone perform *vayati.*"

The entire Council burst into shocked, angry hisses that reminded me of hawks launching from trees.

"You're telling me," said Lord Raksha, "that you can't even use magic?" He finally looked away from me, glaring instead at Devendra. "Is this a joke, Commander Zakir?"

Devendra's hands were balled into fists. "How dare you pin this on me, Raksha," he snarled. "I subdued an entire rebellion to capture Reya Kandhari. Don't tell me you expected me to find her a damn magic guru, too."

"Insolence!" Lord Raksha said. "The Council will be making a report of this to your father."

Devendra stiffened, glaring at me like everything was my fault. I could tell from the way his fingers twitched that he'd love nothing more than to strangle me.

"There's no need to make a report," someone said sharply. I turned to see Sharati looking up at Raksha. She pulled back her veil so he could see her catlike face. "I can train the girl in magic, if his Majesty so desires."

"That's a hell of an offer, Lady Sharati," said Lord Raksha. "However, there are only six weeks remaining until the ceremony."

"That is for me to worry about," said Sharati. "I will ensure that the Bookweaver is prepared to serve his Majesty."

"Will you?" said Raksha, looking unconvinced. "This girl is even more of a disappointment than I had feared. Perhaps we should have stuck with her father."

I felt myself go cold. "What did you say?" My voice frigid, deadly calm.

The quiet before a storm.

One of the lords glanced carelessly at me. "That's not your concern," he said.

The cold was so deep it burned. It felt like icy fire.

"Like hell it's not," I said. "What did you do to my father?"

Raksha frowned. "Your father," he said, "was an insolent wreck. We thought he was a smart man, that he'd cooperate when we showed up at that cottage, but he soon outlived his purpose to us. As such, we decided to speed up the process of transferring his powers to you. We hoped you would be more reasonable."

"You murdered my father," I said, "because you couldn't break him." The air was growing painfully hot around me. "And I swear to god, you won't break me, either."

I could not focus on anything except my incandescent fury: my bones ached and my lungs felt like they could split. Something ignited under my skin—I was consumed.

Below me, the mirrored mosaic trembled ominously, tinkling with eerie musicality. There was a rumbling—the room was pulsing in time with my heartbeat—then the fury burst free, and the floor erupted.

Devendra shoved me out of the way in time, but the mosaic beneath me wasn't spared. Glass shattered within the massive tiled Z, forming a deep crater that glinted with razored shards.

"Stop fighting!" he shouted as I struggled against his grasp, still reaching wildly for Lord Raksha.

"You will not break me!" I shouted, with a mad laugh I didn't know I had in me. "I will break your mosaics—I will break everything—you will not—"

Lady Sharati and Devendra each seized me by an arm, overcoming their mutual hatred in a joined attempt to subdue me. I kicked my legs fruitlessly as they dragged me out of the Council.

Just before Sharati slammed the wooden doors shut, I caught a glimpse of her raising her arms, causing the mosaic to magically sew itself back together.

It was only when we were nearing my chambers that Sharati gathered herself to speak again.

"*What did you do?*" she cried. "You are incredibly close to being killed, as it is. You'll be lucky if your friend Nina survives the night."

I gaped at her, unable to process. "No," I said. "No, I didn't mean for that to happen—"

"Good night, Bookweaver," she snarled, shutting the chamber doors on my face.

There is no point in crying when there is nobody to comfort you. There is no point in crying when guilt unfurls in your chest, reminding you that you don't deserve to be comforted anyway.

In the wardrobe in the bathroom, I found piles of nightclothes—silk gowns, cotton robes. I selected one at random and pulled it on. I noticed that my hair, so elegantly brushed back by Kira, had become disheveled and limp. *Little girl,* Raksha had called me.

That, at least, was a problem I could solve.

There was a pair of paring scissors in the wardrobe. I held the scissors up to my hair, relishing the thrill of cold metal against my skin. Then I closed them around a strand, watching dark brown hairs fall like ash. I took another fistful and snipped. Then another. And another.

As I cut my hair, I thought about my guilt. I imagined it as a little worm—a pale, wriggling thing I had adopted in my heart the day my father died. I'd managed to keep the worm at bay, but now it was preying on me, growing juicy and fat. If I didn't kill it soon, it would devour me until there was nothing left.

When I was finished, I was standing on a carpet of my own hair. My hair, now cropped, rested defiantly around my chin. Strong. Powerful.

I dropped the scissors and left the bathroom, not bothering to sweep. My eyes had fallen on the shelf of books towering over the desk.

The books were bound in leather and velvet, their spines embossed with jewelled hinges. They reminded me of my father. I thought briefly about his book of Kasmiri mythology, lost somewhere in Bharata—probably burned to ashes with the rest of the city. The last memory of him I had left.

I remembered the days my father and I sat in the library, surrounded by castles of books. Candlelight ebbed and flowed as he turned the pages—pages that were yellowed and brittle, but full of words that sang.

"Books are like our friends," he once told me. "They don't backstab. They listen. They heal by whispering words that outlive even time." He'd smiled at me. "And if the book you need doesn't exist, *write it.*"

Without realizing it, I had pulled one of the notebooks off of the shelf and found a blank page. My quill moved, almost involuntarily, to print the book's title.

Ink Soul

I'd never finished anything I started writing. My father had written dozens of books—books that once filled shelves all over Kasmira before they were burned by the Zakirs. He had promised me that one day, I would weave my own words, and that they'd make him proud.

I dipped my quill in the ink and poised it over the paper, letting a single drop splash onto the edge of the page.

It was time to kill that worm.

In the kingdom over blue waters, a dream vibrated through the land.

The words seemed to appear on the page by themselves.

It shone with the sun when it rose, and stayed gleaming like candles in the dark. It was a girl's dream that the kingdom would be free.

As I stared at the text sprawled across the page, I was overcome by familiarity. This wasn't just any story.

The girl was powerful, but she was afraid. Fear clung to her heart like mold, and the sun never warmed the darkest corners of her mind. The girl carried a piece of a dead man's heart inside of her. She was filled with scraps of wisdom gained from the spaces between his words—the moments when he wasn't trying to teach her anything except how to live. It was a crushing burden.

This story was mine.

And so the girl set out on a journey. It was not just a journey to flee the king whose evil knew no bounds, nor was it one to avenge the father she had lost.

Right before sleep overtook me, I scrawled down another line.

It was a quest to discover herself.

Thirteen

I woke up with a scream.

For a moment, all I could do was gasp, trying to erase the distorted visions of my nightmare—Nina, standing alone in the mirrored Council, fire raining down. Devendra, pointing at Jahan's throne, which was no longer empty, but filled by another man—a gruesome corpse with brown hair and green eyes the same shade as mine—

"Reya?"

The door swung open and Kira Chadav burst into the room, balancing a *chai* tray on her hip. She caught sight of me, shivering at the desk where I had fallen asleep, and I saw her eyes widen in concern. "Are you okay? I heard you screaming from the hallway."

I took a deep breath.

"I'm fine," I managed. "I just—nightmare, I think."

Kira set the *chai* tray on the dresser and poured me a steaming cup. "This was meant for Devendra's

133

breakfast, but I think he can spare a cupful for the Bookweaver," she said with a smile. She sat on the side of my bed and waited expectantly as I took a sip.

"This is incredible," I said at last. And it was. The gingery *chai* blossomed in my throat, tracing a warm path down to my stomach.

"Anything I can do for you," said Kira gently. Her expression turned more serious. "Would you like to talk to me about it?"

I tried for a smile.

"I'll be fine," I said. "It's just ... my best friend, Nina. I don't know where she is, but I know she's suffering, and it kills me. She's all I have."

Kira's smile was understanding. "I heard about her," she said. "And I can only imagine how you're feeling. I have a brother, Naveen, who works in the library. He's all I have, too. I know what I'd feel if something happened to him."

She pushed her bright brown hair out of her eyes and glanced at the door, as if to check that the hallway was empty. "But between the two of us, from what I've heard, your friend is a lot stronger than you think."

Kira fell silent as her fellow servants, Trisha and Sita, filed into the room, bearing fresh linens.

"Thank you," I said quietly, so only she could hear. "For the *chai* and for the sympathy."

She was already clearing away my cup. "Come on," she said softly, with only a smile to acknowledge what I had said. "If you get up now, I'll even ask the girls to let you bathe yourself."

In spite of everything, as I hastened to get dressed, I wondered whether I had actually made my second friend in life.

Lady Sharati was irate when she came to receive me—Devendra was sent to accompany her, an arrangement which neither of them seemed pleased with. We made a strange trio—Sharati, veiled and fuming; me, nervously stumbling over my *sari*; Devendra, moodily clenching his sword.

The soldiers at the doorway bowed respectfully as we entered a grand room, designated by embossed golden letters to be the library. I felt my pulse quicken with excitement.

The library was warm and musty, rays of dust slanting through the ceiling windows. Mosaics shattered the light overhead into a million prismatic hues, highlighting the towering rows of bookshelves. Past the archways I could see rows of manuscripts, colorful like jewels, spiraling into the light.

Devendra rolled his eyes, unimpressed. "It's a library," he said. "Quit ogling. If you're the Bookweaver, you ought to get used to seeing *books*."

I ignored him, watching instead as Sharati raised her arms, causing a table to soar through the air and land neatly in front of me.

"Have a seat, Bookweaver," she told me. "It's time to begin your magical training."

I sat down, and she took a seat across from me, steepling her hands before her.

"As you're aware by now, the king wants you to weave a spell for him that will strengthen his power over Kasmira," Sharati said. "In order to awaken your Yogi state, you need to build your magical stamina by becoming proficient in spell-casting."

Devendra stared at her. "Speak Kasmiri, will you?" he snapped.

Sharati huffed. "Reya is the Bookweaver," she explained impatiently. "As such, she has two sets of powers. She has the ability to cast spells, like I do. But as the Bookweaver, she also has the power to perform *vayati,* or weave her words to life."

The crown prince looked irritated. "We all get that part," he interrupted. "But what's the Yogi state?"

"It's not a *what,*" said Sharati haughtily. "It's a *where.* It's a level of magical consciousness and meditation that most Yogis are lucky to achieve even once in their lifetime."

Devendra looked more confused than ever, so I took the opportunity to cut across. "You're saying that I have the power to perform *vay*—whatever you just said—"

"*Vayati,*" said Sharati irately. "It's the Ancient Kasmiri term for 'Bookweaving.' There are only three rules to perform *vayati.* The words must be in Ancient Kasmiri, you must be in your Yogi state, and whatever you do, your *vayati* cannot bring you personal gain."

"Ancient Kasmiri?" I echoed blankly.

"It's a nearly extinct tongue that harnesses magic," someone said from behind me. "It's the only language on earth that's strong enough to carry the power of *vayati.*"

I turned to see a boy appear from behind a shelf. The first thing that struck me was his copper-bright hair. The next thing I noticed were his eyes: they were a thousand colors at once, iridescent like diamonds in the light.

He nodded politely at Lady Sharati. "You called for me, my lady?"

"Sit down, Chadav," Sharati told him. "You're fluent in Ancient Kasmiri, aren't you?"

The boy didn't respond at first: his eyes had landed on Devendra, before moving over to me. I saw the gem-coated pupils widen in shock.

"I'm self-taught," he said, recovering himself. "I've studied every piece of Ancient Kasmiri literature that we have in this library, my lady."

Lady Sharati nodded. "That'll do. You'll be helping me train the Bookweaver, in that case. You can start by documenting her progress for the king."

His eyebrows rose. "I—wow. The Bookweaver. Okay."

He offered me a hand. "Naveen Chadav," he said. "Scribe of the royal library."

I shook his hand, realizing with a jolt that he was the brother Kira had mentioned. "Reya Kandhari," I replied, echoing him. "Bookweaver."

His lip quirked up in a half-smile.

Devendra scoffed impatiently. "There will be plenty of time for introductions later, Kandhari," he snapped. "Right now, my father's got you on a tight schedule."

I glared at him. "So your daddy wants me to perform *vayati* for him," I said. "But I don't even know how to cast normal spells, let alone awaken my Yogi state."

Sharati nodded. "Which is why you'll begin with basic incantations," she said. "The only way your Yogi state can be unlocked is if you take control of your own magic. And judging by what happened yesterday, you've got a long way to go."

"All right," I interrupted, ignoring her needling. "What's the first spell, then?"

"Today, you will be learning the levitation spell," Sharati said. She pulled a mango leaf from within her robes and placed it on the table.

"Magic can be extremely taxing," she warned me. "Casting a spell that's too strong can lead to the death of a Mage. This leaf, however, is easy enough to levitate so we don't need to worry about that happening."

Devendra snickered, and I tried my best to tune him out. "I understand," I said. "Whenever I've used magic without meaning to, I've nearly passed out from exhaustion afterwards."

Beside me, Naveen gave a small gasp of awe.

"A rookie mistake," said Sharati snappishly. "Now, we will begin with the incantation."

She nodded at Naveen, who opened one of the massive books. "This book is called *Bhasa Pratana*," he said, almost reverently. "It translates to *An Ancient Language*, and it contains all the Ancient Kasmiri spells a Mage—or Bookweaver—could ever need."

I peered at the yellowed page to see lines of spiky symbols that I couldn't decipher. The marks were strangely distorted, yet they seemed to whisper. Suddenly, I realized that I was seeing true Ancient Kasmiri—the archaic language that transformed the landscape of Father's oldest books.

"This is the Runic Code," Naveen explained. "Ancient Kasmiri is written in pictographs, with each rune representing a spell. The rune you will need today," he added, running his fingers over the script, "is this one."

"*Rev*," murmured Sharati at the sight of the rune.

"Rise," Naveen translated for my benefit, already taking notes.

Sharati stretched out her long spidery fingers. "I'm going to demonstrate," she told me, "and you will perform the spell after me."

The Mage closed her eyes and raised her hands over the leaf. Out of the corner of my eye, I saw Devendra, despite himself, lean in to watch.

"*Rev*," Sharati breathed, so softly I nearly missed it.

It all happened simultaneously—a breeze of pure energy washed over the table, sending the pages of *Bhasa Pratana* rippling. The leaf billowed slightly, then wafted into the air. Within a moment, it was suspended above our heads, as though the air beneath it had solidified.

Lady Sharati opened her eyes, and the leaf plummeted, landing in front of me. She nodded expectantly, and I felt my fingers freeze up.

Remembering what she had done, I took a deep breath and placed my hands over the leaf, hoping I didn't look as stupid as I felt. I glanced around at my tablemates—Naveen looked excited, Devendra bored, Sharati impatient.

"*Rev*," I said clearly.

Nothing happened.

The leaf remained resolutely still—I'd have been better off blowing at it, for all the reaction I got.

I took another deep breath and reached within myself. I struggled to root into the magic I had once felt entwined with my veins, carved from my marrow and resolute as windfall. But this time, I was empty. I couldn't find my magic.

"*Rev*," I muttered, and this time, I felt a tingle in my lower stomach. The leaf shuddered, but then the power subsided, leaving me more frustrated than before—

"It isn't working. I don't know what's wrong—" I started, but Sharati's face contorted. "What's wrong is *you*, Bookweaver! You're not trying hard enough!"

That stung. I felt the heat rising in my face, and I squeezed my eyes shut.

I knew what magic felt like—the rush, like a shot of sugar in my veins, concentrated at my fingertips, pulsing in my bones. But no matter how hard I concentrated, my fingers felt deadened, my body so tensed that I felt, for all the world, like I was trying to lay an egg. *"Rev,"* I said. *"Rev!"*

Devendra banged the table, causing Naveen to jump.

"What's wrong with her?" he shouted. "I'm responsible to my father if she fails. I know she's done it before, so why can't she make anything happen now—"

"Let's see you do it, then," I countered, but Sharati interrupted.

"Enough," she said. "I think I understand now. You see, Zakir, we have only personally witnessed Reya produce magic under two circumstances. What was the common factor in both cases?"

Devendra rolled his eyes. "I don't know. We were about to arrest her the first time, and she was screaming at the Council the second time. So unless there's some secret factor only you freaks are susceptible to—"

His brow furrowed, all contempt gone. "Unless you mean—both times, she was really angry."

"Exactly. Maybe Miss Kandhari's magic has only emerged under extreme emotional duress," said Sharati. She paused, letting her words sink in—I hated the fact that they were both speaking about me as though I wasn't there. "So clearly, there's only one way to do this."

I don't know what scared me more: the evil smile on her face, or the fact that Devendra seemed to be agreeing with her.

He winked at me, sending chills down my spine. "We raise the stakes," he said.

"Where are we going?" I demanded as Devendra led me through another dark passage. We had descended so many flights of stairs that my legs felt like liquid.

Lady Sharati snapped her fingers, illuminating another row of torchlights.

"The first time you produced magic, you were under a lot of pressure," she said quietly. "You didn't fear for yourself, though. You feared for—"

"Nina," I finished. My voice trembled, and I felt my heart landslide. "No. Not Nina. You're not—"

Sharati glanced at me with cold satisfaction. "I knew you'd understand," she said.

Devendra knocked on an enormous iron gate, and a grim soldier opened the door. Sharati half-escorted, half-dragged me into a circular stone room, which I realized was an underground replica of the mirrored Council. I blinked, my eyes adjusting to the poor lighting.

Then the opposite door opened.

"Nina!" I shouted.

She didn't notice me at first. Nina looked as broken as I felt: her face was darkened—whether from dirt or bruises, I couldn't tell. Then she turned and saw me, and her gray eyes lit up. I felt my heart skip a beat and swell with relief.

"Reya?"

For a moment, I forgot about Devendra and Sharati and all of the soldiers surrounding us. The world faded, and it was just me and my best friend. I crossed the room in two strides, hugging her more tightly than I ever had before, because somehow, we had beaten the odds once again. We were both alive, and that was more than I had hoped for.

Sharati nodded briskly, and the soldiers ripped Nina away before either of us had a chance to protest. "Wait," I said frantically. "Where are you taking her?"

I lunged towards Nina, but Sharati shouted, "*Ilumino!*"

My shoulder collided against a blast of solid air, sending me skidding backwards. Nina's mouth was moving, but I couldn't hear her through Sharati's invisible barrier—only my own ragged breathing, and Devendra's cruel laughter—

"This is your chance," said Sharati coolly. "You will master the levitation spell, or Nina will die."

I turned in horror to see Nina standing in the center of the room, just as the stone floor turned to wax, beginning to froth and melt. Nina's toes disappeared, and then her ankles, and slowly, before my eyes, my best friend was sinking into the floor.

"Stop it!" I said. "You don't have to do this to Nina—"

She shrugged impassively, making it clear that Nina's fate was in my hands now. If I couldn't levitate Nina out of the floor, she would drown.

My pulse pounded in my ears. Already Nina's shins had disappeared from view; she was writhing, but it only served to quicken the stone vortex—*knee-deep, thigh-deep*—

"*Rev!*" I gasped, but all I could feel was my own heart, beating nauseatingly fast. "Come on!" shrieked Sharati, but I barely heard her. Nina was screaming silently from across the room—*chest-deep, neck-deep*—

I closed my eyes and took a deep breath.

And I felt it—the spark, fizzling deep in my bones—and I opened my mouth to utter the spell, but all that came out was a wordless scream, impossible to control. Fire spewed out of my core, and I felt the invisible wall collapse.

The floor around Nina rumbled—she clambered free, covered in ash. Meanwhile, the floor was beginning to crack, and a dull ringing filled my ears.

My throat burned as I gasped for air—the fire was rolling, erupting in waves from the crack in the floor. The ringing amplified, echoing in my head. I clapped my hands over my ears, struggling to make it stop—

Sharati waved her hands through the air, and the fissure in the floor sealed itself. She pointed a finger at me, and an enormous gust of wind blasted me backwards, putting out my fire. I stumbled to my feet.

Nina's guards were dragging her out of the room. I reached for her, but I was stunned by a burst of pain across my cheek—Sharati had slapped me.

"Why can't you focus?" she said. "It was a simple incantation, *and you still managed to blow up the cellar.*"

Fatigue was pulsing through me, but I forced myself to stay upright. "I don't know," I snarled. "I can't—"

To my horror, she pulled the mango leaf from her robes, throwing it at my feet.

"Levitate it now," she ordered. "Use your magic, or I swear to the gods, I will kill Nina myself."

I felt my body shutting down, but I took one last deep breath. "*Rev,*" I muttered, before my knees buckled.

The leaf shot up in the air, uncontrollably fast. Right as I passed out, I saw the leaf burst into flames, like

Kasmira's smallest firecracker. Fleetingly, I imagined the *mahal* bursting into flames—Devendra cursed fluently as the leaf's ashes fell like snow.

Fourteen

Sweat trickled down my brow as I paced my chambers—thirty steps north, thirty steps back.

It almost felt like a fever was pulsing through my body—I couldn't concentrate on anything else as the magic raged through me, pent-up and tingling, keeping my blood awake.

Thirty steps north, thirty steps back.

Random bursts of fire had been escaping me all afternoon, sending stabs of magic through my fingertips. The problem was, the angrier I got, the more uncontrollable my magic became.

Earlier, I had woken from a haze of exhaustion to see the noon sun high over the window. When I tried to get up, I saw that the bed was marred by burns in the precise shape of my hands. I struggled to rein in the magic, but I couldn't—a ceramic vase across the room had been the next to explode. One of the *saris* even caught fire before I managed to stamp it out with my shoes.

Now, as I sat on the floor, my breath calmed to quiet sobs. Because yet again, I had failed Nina. I had failed myself. I had failed my father.

There was a quiet knock on the door. I looked up and saw Naveen Chadav framed in the doorway. He was still holding his notes—as he surveyed the damage, his grip tightened on the pad.

"Can I come in?"

"I guess," I said. "Not really ready for visitors, but—"

He stepped delicately over the broken vase and perched himself carefully on the edge of the bed. "Impressive," he said. "Which army just invaded this place?"

I glared at him, but my heart wasn't in it. "What do you want?"

Naveen wiggled his notebook. "Duty calls," he said. "Sharati wants a full report on your condition to present to his Majesty."

He caught sight of my expression and smiled. "You know, the other scribes are drawing dice on who gets my job if you blow me up," he said. "You're all anyone is talking about."

"All good, I hope," I muttered, and he chuckled.

"I wouldn't hear a word against you," he promised, opening his notebook to a blank page. I watched as he fished a pen from his pocket. "Okay then," he said. "How are you feeling?"

"How do you *think* I'm feeling?" I said dully, indicating the mess around me. His lip twisted up again. "Fair enough," he said. "I'm going to write 'under the weather' and call it a day."

"Under the weather?" I said. "That's an understatement."

Naveen chuckled. "Are you always this chipper, Bookweaver?" His quill flew with an intense speed across the paper that reminded me forcefully of my father. I swallowed painfully.

"I've seen better days," I said.

His quill didn't stop moving, but I could sense his gaze on me. Something about him unnerved me—it was like his diamond eyes could see right through me. Although he wasn't older than sixteen, the depth of his gaze made him seem a thousand years older.

"What?" I said, too defensively.

Naveen looked startled. "Nothing," he said. "You just—you seem broken."

I glared at him. "Don't tell me you're surprised," I said sullenly. "I just watched my best friend get tortured."

Naveen looked shocked. "I had no idea they were allowed to do that to her," he said agitatedly. "I thought his Majesty would never permit such a thing—"

I couldn't prevent the derisive laugh from escaping my lips.

"Where have you been for the past seven years?" I said. "Jahan and Devendra killed hundreds of people in Bharata to capture me. They drove the Mages to the ends of the earth. Trust me, a little bit of torture is nothing for them."

His eyes were wide. "They said those people in Bharata were terrorists," he said quietly.

My blood began to tingle again. "You're wrong," I choked out. "Everything the king has told you is a lie. They weren't terrorists. They were innocent, brave citizens. *And Jahan murdered them.*"

The magic was roaring with emotion. Before I could warn Naveen, it had ripped free from my veins—

I seized my forehead as starbursts of pain ricocheted through my skull.

Naveen's notepad burst into flames. For a moment he was frozen, the burning pad still in his hand.

I knocked the notepad out of his hand, nearly searing myself. He kicked it aside with a yelp. A tongue of flame quickly spread up the side of the bed, trapping Naveen.

"Hang on," I gasped, knocking aside a chair in my haste to reach the bath chamber. I seized a pail at random and thrust it into the bath, spilling a quarter of the water as I tripped over my *sari* hem—

I would have missed it if it wasn't for the mirror over the bath.

In the mirror over the bath, I caught a glimpse of Naveen's reflection, his vivid hair nearly indistinguishable from the deadly fire. He slowly raised his hands, and I saw the spilled water obey him, ebbing gently into the fire, creating a line of hissing ashes.

I dropped the pail, sending water gushing across the bath tiles.

"Wait. Did you just—"

Naveen quickly lowered his hands. "What?" he said casually, but the terror on his face was as good as a confession.

"You just controlled that water," I said. "The fire was about to burn you, but you put it out with your hands. You're a Mage."

The blood rushed back into his face. "I have to go," Naveen muttered, backpedaling frantically towards the door.

"Wait!" I shouted. I slammed the door shut, trapping Naveen inside. He jumped at the noise.

"I don't think—" he started, but I interrupted. A crazy, wonderful idea occurred to me.

"Naveen, can you help me?"

He frowned. "What do you mean?"

"You're exactly the person I need right now," I said excitedly. "I want you to teach me to control magic like you can."

Naveen was shaking his head violently. "I don't think you understand," he said. "Magic is illegal. If you told anybody about me, I could be banished."

"Until yesterday, I was the most wanted person in the country," I said. "Do you really think I'm in a rush to turn you into the king?"

His expression flickered. "Point taken," he said, but then he sighed. "Believe me, I want to be able to practice in the open. More than anything," he said. "But we could get into so much trouble—"

"Fine. We'll make a deal," I told him. "If you teach me magic when you're supposed to be writing your report, I won't tell anyone you're a Mage."

Naveen appraised me, and for a moment, I was afraid he was going to refuse. But then, surprisingly, his lip curled up.

"Am I being blackmailed?"

"It sounds bad when you put it like that," I admitted. "But I swear I'll keep your secret. Bookweaver's honor."

He sighed. "Fine," he said. "What do you want me to teach you?"

"Everything," I said. "Please, everything you know. I've never met another Mage my age before. "

"Neither have I," Naveen said. "For the longest time, I was alone. I thought I was going insane."

I frowned. "But I thought magic was hereditary. Nobody in your family was a Mage?"

"Usually it runs in the family," he agreed. "For me, it was my mother."

"Your mother?" I prodded.

"She died a long time ago," he said. "So she wasn't much help to me."

I could sense there was more to the story, but I didn't want to press him, not when I could hear the pain in the edges of his voice. "Mine, too," I murmured.

His eyes crinkled in sympathy. "Anyway, I found my magic at a young age. It's always been natural to me. I had a way with water. It obeyed me."

He saw my questioning glance and smiled. "It's easier to show you."

Naveen pointed a hand, almost lazily, at the puddle of water I'd spilled on the floor. And then the water rose at his command, forming a shimmering wall. As he inhaled and exhaled, the water mirrored him, ebbing and rippling like a translucent ribbon, conduits twisting neatly back into the pail.

"That was unbelievable," I managed. "How did you learn to do all of that?"

Naveen shrugged modestly.

"It took a lot of practice," he said. "When our mother died, Kira and I moved to the *mahal*. Being a scribe had its benefits, because I could learn as much as I wanted from the library. I read *Bhasa Pratana* cover to cover until I could speak Ancient Kasmiri."

His face fell slightly. "It's been hard, staying hidden," said Naveen. "I haven't told anyone about my magic, except Kira."

The thing was, I understood.

I understood him with more clarity than I had ever understood anything in my life. Nobody had ever been able to talk about this with me—not even Nina. I hadn't realized how badly I needed him until Naveen was sitting before me, holding the key to my identity in his hands.

I didn't tell Naveen this, though—I kept my voice steady, as though I was used to meeting Mages every other day. "How do you do it?" I asked. "How do you control your power like that?"

"Using magic is different for everyone," Naveen explained. "It's like your fingerprint. My way works on my magic. You have to find a way to control it so that it doesn't control you."

I liked the way he talked—he was unabashedly intellectual, and he spoke like a book.

"Well, judging by how today went," I said, "I don't think I'm there yet."

"I couldn't control myself at first, either," admitted Naveen. "But then I found my anchor."

"Your anchor?"

He blushed a little. "I don't know if this is how actual Mages do it," Naveen said. "But whenever I felt like the magic was drowning me, I reminded myself I could beat it. I remembered someone who *made me* want to beat it. Someone who was strong enough to anchor me when things got hard."

"Kira," I said.

"Kira," he agreed. "I don't know why I got the magic gene, and my sister didn't. But she's always been there for me, pulling me back from the edge every time."

He smiled. "What about you? Who anchors you?"

I felt an uncomfortable pit in my stomach. All of a sudden, I was acutely aware of just how lonely I was.

"I have nobody," I said hollowly. I didn't mean to sound so plaintive, but the words escaped me, painfully childlike. I couldn't meet Naveen's eyes—instead, I stared at the burned carpet.

"I wouldn't say *nobody*," said Naveen quietly.

I glanced up at him. There was still a faint trace of a smile on his face, but his eyes were serious. "I can help you," he said. "I can anchor you. I can teach you to find your magic."

"Please," I said. "I barely know you. In the last ten minutes I've screamed at you, nearly scorched you, and then blackmailed you."

"Regrettably," said Naveen. "But even if your manners leave much to be desired, you're the only other Mage I've ever met in my life. That's not nothing to me."

In spite of everything, I smiled. I knew what it felt like to be surrounded by people who could never really see you. I knew the alienation that came from feeling completely out of place. I knew the fear that the people who loved you might end up hurt—or worse—if you ever became who you truly needed to be.

And so did he. He was complex in ways only I could ever understand. It was an enormous relief. But for now, I let myself drift into the moment, softly, like an evening candle. I let that be enough.

He looked back at me. Something deep shifted inside, maybe for both of us, and I took a deep breath.

"Okay," I said. "How do we start?"

Naveen grinned. "Sit down on the mattress and close your eyes."

I did, and I felt his hands take mine. "Just breathe,"

he said. "And when you do, I want you to find my magic. And I'll find yours."

I felt myself relax, inhaling and exhaling. The magic within me was bubbling, painfully hot, but Naveen's hands were cool on mine. His presence, strange and wonderful, seemed to expand around us.

"Are you ready?" Naveen murmured. I nodded, and he said, "On three, then?"

"One," I whispered. I felt the heat releasing me. It felt like peeling off dirty clothes and stepping into a cool bath.

"Two." His powers, deep and serene, seemed to bend the room around him. He didn't extinguish my fire—he harnessed it. He kept the rage at bay.

"Three," he finished, and I said, "*Rev.*"

It was like there was another force—another world, another dimension—in the tiny space between our hands. I could feel my magic, fiery and turbulent, layering against Naveen's, steady and constant, like deep ocean currents.

I opened my eyes as all around us, the pillows bobbed into the air, floating like clouds. Even the mattress beneath us had risen a foot above the ground. In that moment, we were suspended in midair. We were floating.

Naveen released my hand, and the mattress fell with a thump.

"How did it feel?" he asked.

I couldn't contain the grin spreading across my face. "Like I was finally alive," I said. "I didn't know what I was missing all this time."

His lip turned up again in that inscrutable half-grin. "That's how it's supposed to feel," he said. "Your

magic isn't supposed to be driven by rage or hate or
fear. It's pure."

He was right. For the first time, my magic belonged
to me. I felt it like a violent seed within me, finally
allowed to softly blossom, and I realized that I'd had
power over it all along.

"All right, guru," I said. "What's next?"

From up in the *mahal*, the Fields were a faraway blur
of grass, an embroidered rug flung onto the horizon.
Wrapped in a shawl against the recent chill, I wondered which girl was gathering mangoes in my place.

Even as summer waned, melting and cooling into
autumn, I felt my own magic reshaping itself each day.
It was almost laughable to think that raising a leaf had
once been a challenge. With Naveen's support, I finally
gained control over my magic. From levitation I pro-
gressed to locomotion, summoning, and conjuring with
an ease that even Sharati had a hard time criticizing.

Still, as I gazed out of my window, I grappled with
the realization that there was nowhere else to run,
nobody left to be. I would remain cloistered in the
mahal, even as a thousand summers turned into a
thousand falls, facing the terrible truth that I belonged
to someone else.

I could see my desperation reflected in *Ink Soul*.
Although I had poured out chapters, poems, and
vignettes, the opening story eluded me. Every night
when I sat down to write, I reread those first lines about
the kingdom over blue waters, hoping for the rest of the
words to come. But inevitably, I turned the page.

It was on a clear golden morning with leaves falling like rain that Lady Sharati finally broached the subject of *vayati.*

Instead of the library, our party of four had convened in a vast hall. Devendra glowered at me as I ran through my warm-ups.

Sharati wasn't watching me with her usual haughty sneer—instead, she seemed almost nervous. When I was finished, she pulled out a piece of purple parchment.

"This is an order from his Majesty," she told me. "He's been reviewing your progress and thinks it's time you prepare to perform *vayati.*"

I frowned. "Why haven't I seen him yet?"

There had been no sign of Jahan since he had failed to appear before the Council. It was like the king was invisible.

Devendra looked annoyed. "My father is a busy man. He has a kingdom to run."

"And what about you?" I taunted. "You're the imperial commander of Kasmira. Don't you have anything better to do than babysit me?"

He scowled. "Shut up."

I smiled at him. "You sound bitter. Has your father been giving you the cold shoulder, too?"

I stretched my arms behind me. "It seems to me like we're both getting the same amount of attention from our fathers. And mine's dead."

Sharati cut across. "Quit bickering," she said. "We're running out of time. You need to be prepared to perform *vayati.*"

"And how exactly do I do that?" I asked. "All you've told me is that I need to unlock my Yogi state."

"You'll be able to unlock it during the actual ceremony," said Naveen. "Lady Sharati can't simulate it beforehand. That's too much power to subject you to without actually performing *vayati*."

"In other words, we don't want to kill you too soon," said Sharati cheerlessly.

"I feel valued," I said, and Naveen grinned furtively into his notebook.

"In the meantime," Sharati said, ignoring my comment, "there's another spell you can practice that will prepare you for how exhausting *vayati* feels. The technique is simple, but it's the most taxing spell there is."

"You'll be raising a Shield," said Devendra.

"A Shield?"

"It's a magical protection," explained Naveen, sounding, as usual, like he'd swallowed a spellbook. "It causes your opponent's spell to rebound against them. It's very hard, because you have to control your own power in addition to theirs."

"Also, there's no incantation," said Sharati. "It's a spontaneous expression of power. You have to be ready at any moment."

At her command, I started toward the opposite side of the room to practice.

I felt Sharati's magic before I heard it. Without warning, she raised her arms. "*Aquine!*" she screamed.

I whirled around to see a bolt of freezing water spiraling from her palms, moving so fast that it looked like a blur. I ducked just in time, but the next jet hit me squarely in the face, sending me reeling.

"What was that for?" I said angrily.

Devendra sneered. "You didn't Shield," said Sharati accusingly. "I told you that you had to be ready."

"I'm sorry," I snarled. "It's a little hard to focus

when you keep trying to drown me." I bit my lip to contain its shiver.

"Quit complaining. It's supposed to be taxing. Try again," commanded Sharati.

She reared back, and I bent my knees in anticipation. This time, I was ready.

I felt the power building inside me, swirling in my hands. As the first hints of water splashed me, I released it all at once. And then Sharati's magic collided with mine.

"Taxing" was an understatement.

The pressure made me feel like I was trapped between two hard and unyielding jaws, slowly being crushed. I clenched my fists and watched the water splay against my invisible Shield—it rocketed back towards Sharati.

Quick as lightning, she raised her arms and the water changed directions. It bounced off her own Shield so rapidly that I barely had time to react before I was hit for a second time. I fell flat on my back.

"Not quick enough!" I heard Sharati saying. "Again!"

I rolled out of the way and onto my feet as the fourth bolt of water struck the ground next to me. She waved her hands and the water rose into a column like Naveen's had done. Except while Naveen's magic felt gentle and capricious, the water racing towards me looked ready to flatten me—

I was exhausted, but I forced my magic to rise like the water had. I imagined an actual shield, hard as rock, expanding from my fingertips, just as the water collided with me.

The Shield blossomed forth with surprising strength, but nobody seemed more surprised than Lady Sharati herself. The water rebounded with unconquerable force, catching her in the chest. For a moment, she was suspended in the air. Then she collapsed onto the floor.

"Lady Sharati!"

Naveen scurried towards her, looking terrified. I dropped the Shield and rushed to her side, ignoring Devendra's laughter.

When she staggered to her feet, Sharati looked murderous.

"I'm sorry," I started. "That was too powerful—"

I had misread her expression. She wasn't angry. She looked nervous.

"Quiet, Bookweaver," Sharati said, not looking at me. She was making eye contact with Devendra, who had stopped laughing and was nodding grimly.

"Contact your father," she told him. "Let him know it's time."

"Time for what?" I interrupted, but she ignored me. "Chadav, accompany the Bookweaver to her chambers," she said. "This lesson is over."

Fifteen

Ink Soul: Chapter VII

    It was during another autumn of crisp sunshine and golden leaves that Father stepped out of our cottage for the first time in months. Summer passed without a single raid on the Fringes, and Father decided it was time to rejoice.

    "What are we celebrating?" I asked, almost suspiciously. He laughed. "Life," he told me, tweaking my nose. He limped up the stairs to the Firebreath Tavern.

    At first, I hated the Firebreath—the raucous bartenders and uproarious laughter, the filthy glasses, the pounding music, and the cigar smoke that sent my skin crawling. But Father was happy, so I could tolerate it, at least for one night.

    Father ordered me persimmon cider—the only non-alcoholic drink the Firebreath served. I soon discovered the source of the bar's name.

*Firedancers leaped and barreled through flame,
swallowing flickering torches before belching
them up again. The crowd screamed as one,
faces illuminated by the ebbing firelight.*

*I sipped through the dirty glass, but once I got
used to the bitter filth, the cider wasn't bad. It
was tangy and smoke-flavored, but the persim-
mon tasted sweet. And I realized, that this was
everything I had ever wanted—my father and I
safe, happy. In that fleeting, persimmon-flavored
moment, I had found it. In that moment, my
father and I had defeated Jahan Zakir.*

*The drunk band struck up a lively tune—rich
and flowing, snake pipes and* dhol *drums, far
from the flavorless music they played for the priv-
ileged. I'd never paid much attention to music
before, except for the occasional work chant at
the Fields—it was something that belonged to
people who were safer than me. But then, my feet
began to tap to the flamboyant tune.*

*"My fiery girl," crooned the singer. "You are
my flower. You are the flaming flower that sets
my poor heart ablaze ... "*

And then the Bookweaver began to dance.

*He danced with none of the grace he had
long ago, but he danced with all of the fire. He
leapt up and down, his leg trailing, arms whirling like watermills.*

*Dancing unexpectedly—that's how he used
to be. Cracking random jokes, laughing wildly,
making everyone smile—for a moment, it was as
though Jahan had never taken power.*

Around him, people nodded appreciatively.

The air was filled with clinks as people set down their glasses and made their way to the dance floor: some excitedly, others dragged by more intoxicated partners. The night wore on and a group chain formed—round and round went the dancers, my father flying between them. Suddenly his feet were in perfect alignment, his gait not quite so awkward.

He didn't look like the broken Bookweaver. He looked like a man.

Inexplicably, my face was burning. In a rush of fury, I strode through the dance circle, sending people tripping indignantly out of the way.

"What's wrong, Reya?" he began, but I tugged him out the door.

"Who are you, Father?" I snarled, tears tugging at my eyes. "Are you this brave, laughing man, or are you the crippled peasant in the Fringes? Are you a strong leader, or are you a helpless victim?"

He looked aghast, but I wouldn't let him get a word in.

"I don't understand," I said, before I started to cry. "You made all of those people dance. You gave them hope. Why couldn't you do that when it actually counted?"

I saw that I had hurt him, and it gave me satisfaction, in spite of my guilt. I knew he wanted to let me into his world, to understand his story. In that moment, all I wanted to do was write my own.

That's when I first learned about the cosmic laws of karma. The universe has a way of repay-

*ing cruelty. The day after I screamed at him,
Father came down with a fever, and I stayed up
for four nights taking his temperature. During
those sleepless nights, all I could think about was
my guilt.*

*We didn't speak about the incident after that,
but I don't think he ever stopped thinking about
it either.*

I set down the pen, hands shaking slightly. Ink had
stained the inside of my fingers, but nevertheless, I felt
steadier than I had all day. I was determined to get my
father's story onto paper—both the good parts and the
bad ones, the ones that kept me awake at night.

Still, the opening of *Ink Soul* eluded me. Over and
over I read the first line.

In the kingdom over blue waters...

A distraction arrived in the shape of Naveen. I
quickly stuffed the manuscript into my desk drawer.

"How are you holding up?" he asked, flopping onto
my bed.

"Me? I'm fine," I said. "I think the question is, how
is Sharati holding up?"

Naveen chuckled. "Not well. The expression on her
face when you blasted her was priceless."

"Well, she's had it coming for a while," I said. "I
would've loved to accidentally soak Devendra, too."

"He's been on edge," Naveen said darkly. "His
father still hasn't granted him an audience since
Bharata. Devendra's taking it really hard."

"I don't understand," I said. "Devendra is already the

military commander of Kasmira. Why is he so obsessed with his father's honor?"

Naveen gave me a searching look. "You're the Bookweaver's daughter," he said. "Is that really so hard to understand?"

I dropped my gaze. "I guess not," I said. "But he's still crazy."

"Look who's talking," said Naveen, and I threw a pillow at him.

The door burst open, and Lady Sharati and Devendra appeared. The crown prince, as usual, looked bored, but Sharati was almost frenzied.

"Good. You've finished the report," she told Naveen, who nodded hastily. Sharati turned to me. "It's time."

I stood up. "You keep saying that," I said. "Time for what?"

Devendra smiled, and his expression sent a trickle of foreboding down my spine. Lady Sharati frowned slightly. "It's time to have you housebroken, as it were," she said. "We're going to meet the Spider."

Out of the corner of my eye, I saw Naveen stiffen. He caught me looking at him and tried to feign casualness. "In that case, you'd better not be late," he said.

I followed them out of the room, but to my surprise, Devendra didn't lead me down any hallway I recognized. Instead, he turned a corner into a dirty, sunless chamber, marked only by a door. Sharati strode ahead and placed her palm against the knob. I heard the telltale sizzle of magic as the knob turned.

Beyond the door, a twisting staircase tunneled deep into the earth. It smelled dank and foul, as though a creature had recently died down below. When Lady Sharati whispered "Temperus," her voice echoed through the dark hall, illuminating torch brackets in a never-ending spiral.

"You first," I told Devendra, who scowled. He shuffled down the staircase, and I followed him into the bowels of the palace.

Sweat accumulated on my palms as we walked through the pitch-black hallway. I was acutely aware of the sound of my breathing and the click of Sharati's heels on the floor; Devendra alone moved noiselessly. Dark shadows stood sentry along the corridor—I couldn't tell if they were men or statues until one blinked, his white eyes glinting like pearls. Startled, I scuttled straight into Devendra.

A somber servant struck a match and lit the torches in the room. Greasy light ebbed around us.

"It has been a month since his Majesty has started your education. Now, he deems it necessary to take certain precautions," said Lady Sharati. The torches cast shadows on her eyes, making her look like a phantom.

Phantoms aren't real, I told myself nervously: this was just my claustrophobia working on overdrive. The next thing I knew, I would be seeing ghosts.

And then I saw a ghost.

It was tall, slender, glinting with metal. As it passed by, the lanterns flickered, and I felt the temperature drop. Its face was serene as death itself behind a skull-like silver mask, shrouded beneath a black robe. Metal hands extended from its sleeves, but its form rippled, giving the impression that there were six more limbs, coiled tentacle-like beneath its robes.

"Leave that to me, Lady Sharati," it said, its voice like knives against stone. She obeyed immediately, and my flesh crawled as it advanced, but I stood my ground.

"The king's greatest potential enemy … and ally," murmured the creature. It sounded almost humanoid, but not quite; the cruelty in its voice was alien. "So insubstantial … like a wisp of smoke, easily wavering in loyalty."

I could only stare at the darkness beneath its hood. Somehow, I found my voice.

"What are you?"

"I am the Spider," it whispered. "I am the emperor's chief Mage."

Its mouth curved into a ghostly smile.

"You shudder, Bookweaver? I was once human like you. But I sought more than the fragile confines of human life. I may be immortalized into metal, but my spirit lives within. I carry the power of a thousand lives and a thousand deaths."

There was a pregnant silence, broken by Prince Devendra. "My father fears the Bookweaver's disloyalty, now that's she's become more powerful," he told the Spider. "He wants you to curse her magic. Like you cursed her father."

The mention of my father's name was enough to overcome my fear.

"What are you talking about?" I demanded. "*What did you do to my father?*"

"Enough," said the Spider. It raised its metallic hand in the air and I felt my throat close. I struggled to speak but nothing came out—

It smiled coldly. "It appears that the king has a special curse in mind for you," it murmured. "I had the pleasure of performing it on your father before I killed him."

Fury pounded through my blood, and I opened my mouth to yell at him, but my throat was frozen, and Devendra snickered—

"So I shall deliver," the Spider continued. "Should you attempt magic against King Jahan's wishes, my curse will activate. And then, you will find yourself hard-pressed to disobey him."

Before I could react, the Spider raised its limbs. Its voice slithered through my ears. "Let's see if this Bookweaver is made of stronger stuff than her father."

In a metallic flash, the pressure descended on me, concentrated on the pearl around my neck, which burned like fire. My eyes were popping in their sockets, my ears caving inward, a soundless scream fighting to push through my lips.

Then Nina was standing before me. There, but not there, a shimmering projection against the stone wall.

Her face was dark with rage. "Reya," she said, and somehow, she managed to inject those two syllables with more hatred than I thought possible. "A sorry excuse for a friend."

Fury colored her words. "You abused my friendship, destroyed my future, wrecked my every chance for happiness."

Terrible guilt washed through me, and I tried to protest, but Nina cut across. "You're the reason I was forced to live as a fugitive, captured, and nearly killed a thousand times over! It was you!"

This was not the Nina who I loved and trusted, but a creature wearing her face and carrying her voice. Her words tore apart closing wounds, replacing my blood with fire.

"That's not true!" I cried. "I love you, and all I wanted was to save you."

Nina's lips spread into a mocking smile.

"You love me," she repeated, sneering. "You love

me, and yet you couldn't even get it together to save me from Sharati's spell. You dragged me on this suicide mission, and then you abandoned me after you killed your precious father."

Tears stung my eyes. "Wait!" I screamed. But Nina had morphed into another woman: my mother, back from the grave. Kamala Kandhari was more beautiful than I remembered, but more terrible. Her eyes were frigid.

"Mother?"

"Get back," she said, her voice deadly. "I'm not your mother, beast."

She crossed her arms. "I gave birth to a monster, and I regret it every day. I gave up my life to save *you,* a girl who's caused the death of hundreds before her sixteenth birthday."

I bit my lip. "Mom—" I hadn't called her that since I was three. "Mom, come on. It's me, Reya!" But she shook her head.

"This is not the girl I was willing to die for seven years ago," she said dismissively. "The girl I see is a killer and a menace, a tarnish on our family name." She paused. "Except I don't have a family. My husband is gone, thanks to you, and you've long since been dead to me."

My mother turned on her heel and walked away. A scream of frustration escaped my lips—an inhuman, desperate scream—just as another scream blossomed from somewhere to my right.

Roshan was on his knees, pounding on my father's lifeless body. He looked up at me, grief etched on every line of his face. "You killed him!" he screamed. "I loved my brother. He's dead!" My uncle buried his face. "He's all I had! He's all—"

Behind him stood another man—Niam. And next to him— Aisha. Their faces were contorted in rage, covered in the blood of their comrades. "They're all dead!" he shouted. "Hundreds of brave men, for you?" Aisha strung her bow, pointed it at me, and I felt an arrow pierce me, but the physical pain had nothing on the guilt pulsing in my gut—

Devendra stood over me, scowling, and I blinked frantically, tears clouding my vision. "Aisha—" I croaked.

"Get up," Devendra said. "We're done here."

The Spider floated into my periphery, jerking me back to reality.

"What did you do to me?" I demanded. "What did you—"

"The curse is complete," said the Spider calmly. "Cast any spell that defies the king's wishes, and your magic will eat you alive."

"You're getting into my head, making me see things," I snarled. "But they're not true. My friends wouldn't give up on me like that."

The Spider eyed me carefully.

"I conjured those visions, yes. But I didn't make any of that up. I only showed you the darkest fears nestled in your heart. They've been there the whole time."

My breath escaped with a hiss. "Stop toying with me," I said, my voice shaking uncontrollably.

The Spider smiled. "The curse only attacks what already exists," it said. "You know it's true. You know that you bring nothing but pain to those who love you. You take their love and then burn everything in your wake."

I tried to stand, but I couldn't—the curse was burning into my skin. Devendra's face faded, the shadows thickened, and everything went black.

When I woke up, a firebird was singing in the distance.

Around me, our garden grew lushly, perfumed like springtime. Jasmine, my mother's favorite flower, sprouted in all corners, and thick ivy ensnarled the walls. My heartbeat quickened. I was home.

The firebird landed on the edge of the fountain, and I froze, trying my best not to startle it or disturb its song.

"Beautiful, isn't it?" asked a warm voice.

I turned around slowly, not daring to believe my ears.

My mother was strolling along the garden path, wearing an elegant *sari* in the precise color of the jasmine around her. Her brown eyes shone as she walked, her bare feet making indentations in the soft almost-summer earth. She hugged me, and I breathed in the familiar scent of lily perfume.

"Mother?" I whispered.

She smiled at me, and her presence blanketed me like a quilt. "I'm here, Reya," she said. "You know that I'm always here."

Together we watched as the firebird, startled by her voice, opened its small wings in flight. I felt like a weight had been lifted off my shoulders. My mother didn't think I was a beast. How could I have doubted her for a second?

"Reya, you grow lovelier by the instant," she said, and I blushed. She stroked my hair, smiling absently. "Well, come on for lunch. Your father has made the only dish he knows— curried okra and saffron rice. Can you smell it?"

Just then, someone else stepped into the garden. Handsome and carefree, my father tossed back a mane of gray-free hair, as though trying to impress my mother. We exchanged glances, and she waved flirtatiously at her husband.

"Kamala, the feast will be cold soon," he called. He grinned at me and added, on second thought, "Or gone, since I'll have eaten it for you."

Unconsciously, I touched my neck. The pearl was smooth and whole, gleaming with robust light.

"Honestly, Amar," said my mother with mock-severity. "You could eat a mountain and still be hungry. I was just looking at how beautiful our daughter was."

Father looked at me, scrutinizing me from all angles, his dashing features contorting into the most ridiculous expressions. I couldn't help but laugh.

"There it is," he said. "She looks infinitely more beautiful with a smile on." He turned to Mother and took her hand. Together, they strolled towards our bungalow. Mother turned back and extended her free hand invitingly.

"Come on, Reya," she said.

I ran towards her, my hands outstretched, eager to join her once more. Just as my hand reached hers, she disappeared into darkness, and I was floating.

Something brown swam before my eyes, and I reached for it, desperate for something to hold.

"Mother?"

Kira's face materialized before my eyes—the brown was her hair, hanging loosely from her face. I tried to sit up, but the mattress was too soft, and I felt myself sink back into the pillows.

"It's okay," she said softly. "You're safe. You're in

your chambers now. I'm here to watch over you."

"My chambers?" I repeated. "No, I ..."

But even through my sleep-fuddled eyes, I could tell that I wasn't in a garden. Instead, I was in the drafty chamber that I so hated, mid-afternoon sunlight streaming through the window. Despite myself, I felt the familiar pinch behind my eyes.

"You don't understand, Kira. She was right here!"

Kira sighed. "The aftereffects of the curse might have made you hallucinate."

I gestured wildly, trying to make her understand. "She told me that I was beautiful—there was a firebird—"

Kira looked me in the eye, and something in her voice seemed to break me. "Reya, your mother is dead."

She seemed to sense the harshness of her words, because her eyes were soft as she helped me out of the bed. "Naveen told me what the Spider did to you," she said quietly. "I'm sorry. I really am."

I stared at the opposite wall. "Occupational hazard of being the Bookweaver, I guess."

"Still, you were cursed," she said. "I don't know as much about magic as my brother does, but I know it must have been hard. And you survived."

I glanced at her. Kira really did resemble Naveen, with her delicate features and bright brown hair. But where his eyes were multicolored, hers were a flat warm copper.

"We talk so much about me," I said at last. "What about you, Kira?"

She looked surprised. "If Jahan had never taken over," I pressed. "Who would you be? Who would you have wanted to become?"

"I'm not sure," said Kira quietly. She started folding

my sheets, and to my relief, she did not protest when I moved to help her. "Even though working as a palace maid is horrible, I've always loved to serve people. To help make their lives better."

Kira looked at me, and I saw a real smile on her face. "So to answer your question, I think I would've wanted to be a healer."

"A healer," I repeated, tasting the word on my tongue. It was a gentle sort of word. It suited Kira, with her encouraging smiles and small acts of kindness.

"Yeah," she said. "I'd want to be at the Kasmiri-Indiran border, helping people who were hurt, no matter whose side they were on. There are enough fighters in this kingdom. Sometimes, you just need somebody to bind up the wounds."

I thought about all the wounds I had created. Kira was everything I'd always wanted but never managed to be. Because where she was healing and compassionate, I was destructive and vengeful. Would things have turned out differently if Kira was the Bookweaver and I was her servant?

My thoughts were interrupted by a knock on the door. We both looked up to see Lady Sharati standing in the doorway.

"Bookweaver, his Majesty has summoned you to the courtrooms," she said. "We have to leave now."

I glared at her. "Why?"

Sharati pursed her lips. "Because it's time for the hearing," she said. "The hearing of the most infamous traitor Kasmira has ever known. Nina Nadeer."

Sixteen

My foot drummed incessantly against the pew in front of me. Rushes of emotion hit me like waves, staggering and unending—a ripple of nerves; a surge of guilt; an ebb of anger that crested into fear. Because somehow, I couldn't shake the feeling that this might be the last time I ever saw Nina Nadeer.

To calm myself, I thought of what I knew, repeating it like a mantra in my head.

My name is Reya Kandhari. I am the Bookweaver's daughter. Nothing else is what it seems.

With every passing minute, the crowd grew thicker. Soon the pews were filled with nobles, all muttering nervously. I could sense the undercurrent of fear beneath the hushed tones—years of forced peace had been shattered when Bharata rebelled.

To them, Nina was more than just a fugitive. They preferred peace over freedom, so she was a threat.

173

I could see King Jahan's private pew, cloistered in an alcove above the court. He was veiled by a purple curtain, but if I squinted, I could make out his silhouette, like the shadow puppets I'd made with my fingers as a child.

My name is Reya Kandhari. I am the Bookweaver's daughter. Nothing else is what it seems.

A gong sounded, and the entire court went silent. The excitement was palpable as the gong's last vibrations echoed across the room, bouncing against the walls until only the faintest hum remained.

Lord Raksha strode down the pews into the center of the room. His eyes travelled across the courtroom, lingering briefly on me, before he unrolled an enormous sheaf of parchment.

"I present to his Majesty the case of Nina Nadeer," he announced. He glanced up at the lofty pew as he said it, but there was no movement or acknowledgement from the king. Raksha seemed to hesitate for a moment, and he nodded to the soldiers. "Bring her in," he said.

On cue, the doors swung open once more.

I turned towards them eagerly, desperate for a glimpse of Nina. I wasn't alone—there was a collective creaking as the entire courtroom leaned forward in its seats. A dozen armed imperial soldiers marched into the courtroom. Shuffling between them, dwarfed by their enormous weapons, was Nina.

The nobles roared and jeered as one, and Raksha banged the gong halfheartedly to stop them.

My stomach squeezed, because for the first time, Nina didn't look like the unconquerable girl I had always known her to be. From my seat in the pews, she looked gaunt and fragile, smaller than I'd ever seen her before.

I could see her head turning, searching for some-one. At last, her eyes met mine, and their expression was what truly scared me. Her irises were no longer gray. They looked black.

Nina took me in—almost doll-like in my lavish *sari*, surrounded by servants—as I beheld her: bare feet dirty, hair limp, shrunken by oversized robes. Something in her expression was closed off, as though she no longer recognized me.

"The accused has been produced," announced Lord Raksha. He had to shout it several times before the room quieted. "I call upon Prince Devendra Zakir to present the charges."

Devendra stood, and I noticed he was dressed in full military gear: purple turban, glinting lapels, sword sheathed. His cloak billowed impressively behind him as he walked, making him look larger than he was. The soldiers all lowered their heads in respect as he passed.

"As imperial commander of Kasmira, it is my duty and honor to bring this traitor to justice," said Devendra pompously. "The charges against Nina Nadeer are as follows."

He smiled coldly at Nina, who glared back, and I saw the mutual hatred in their eyes. With a shiver, I remembered how Nina had humiliated him in Bharata. Now was his chance for revenge.

The crown prince took Raksha's enormous parch-ment and began reading from the list. "Truancy from the Fields. Evasion of arrest. Assault against my soldiers on numerous occasions. Collusion with public ene-mies. Attempts to undermine the regime."

Each charge struck me like a blow, worsened by the cruel relish in Devendra's voice. He paused delicately, allowing the courtroom to quiet down before he read the final charge.

"Militant insurgence."

The shouts erupted again. Nina looked like she was carved from stone—but I could tell that her shoulders were trembling.

"Miss Nadeer, you are surely aware of what the penalty is for such crimes," Devendra continued silkily. "You're clearly not the brightest, but I know you're not *that* stupid."

Even from fifty pews above, even before Nina opened her mouth, I knew what she was going to do, and I knew I couldn't stop her.

"Oh, I don't know," said Nina with awful coldness. "There's a fine line between stupidity and bravery. Not that I'd expect you to know anything about the latter."

Devendra sneered. "Bravery?" he said. "You call your half-baked little rebellion *bravery?*"

"I do," Nina said. "And it's a hell of a lot braver than threatening an entire city of innocent people, just because you couldn't keep ahold of two peasant girls."

Her voice gained momentum. "You're a coward, Devendra Zakir. You blew up a mountain of better men than you because you couldn't take them head-on. You kicked a defeated city when it was down. You—"

"Shut up!" said Devendra. Whispers rippled through the courtroom, and I saw Devendra redden. He tried for a more placating tone. "Why are you still trying to martyr yourself for a lost cause?"

"Why are you still trying to be your daddy's lapdog?" Nina shot back.

She had touched a nerve. There was a zinging noise as Devendra drew his sword in a rush of fury. "You filthy little peasant—"

"Go ahead," Nina taunted. "Kill me. Prove to your father what a man you are, attacking a girl who's swordless—"

"Enough," Devendra said. His face bypassed red and turned a sickly shade of blue as he shoved his sword away—he missed the sheath in his anger, and the blade clattered to the floor. Embarrassed, he stooped to pick it up.

"You're right. I should kill you," he spat. "But luckily for you, peasant, my father wants to offer you a second chance."

He glanced at the pew where his father sat, but the king said nothing. Devendra faltered for a fraction of an instant, and he wheeled back on Nina.

"If you renounce the Renegades and pledge your loyalty to my father," he said, "his Majesty will welcome you back into the kingdom. No questions asked."

From the renewed whispers in the courtroom, I knew I wasn't the only one who was completely shocked by Jahan's offer.

Down below, Nina looked bewildered. "I don't understand—"

"Renounce the rebellion, and your life will be spared," Devendra said. "My father is not without mercy. You have the power to save millions of lives, including your own, by disavowing the resistance and joining the right side of history."

I saw Nina's shoulders tighten.

"You're asking me to sell out all the people who ever believed in the resistance," she said softly. "This isn't about me. You want to make me a symbol."

Devendra rolled his eyes. "Don't be so dramatic," he said. "You can jump off a sinking ship and live to see another day, or you can drown. This is the choice my father has given you. You should be grateful, Nadeer."

For a moment, Nina was quiet, and even I couldn't fathom what must have been running through her head.

"Why doesn't he ask me himself?" she said at last.

A gasp rippled through the courtroom, just as a soft cough came from high above.

I looked up so fast I cricked my neck, but I still couldn't see the king. Jahan's voice was quiet, barely audible from behind the curtain. Perhaps I was just imagining that I could see a hint of the purple flicker in his eyes.

"Nina Nadeer," he said.

I still can't forget his voice. There was a soothing cadence to the way it shaped Nina's name, caressing every syllable. It was enticing, even understanding. It made me want to trust him. It made me want to obey him with every fiber of my being.

"You're a very special girl, Nina," Jahan breathed, and the familiarity of his compliment made my skin crawl. "Miss Kandhari chose well."

He paused, and I felt the audience's eyes turn on me. "The Bookweaver has made the right choice again. She has joined me, you know. You can, too."

Nina turned to face me, the betrayal darkening her eyes. I felt as though the floor had disappeared beneath me—I wanted to scream that it wasn't true, that I was still hers, but my mouth wouldn't move.

I could see her hesitating. In that moment, I realized that this might be my only chance to undo all the pain that I had caused her over the last seven years.

My heart felt like it was being crushed into a million pieces, but I forced myself to look in her direction.

"Please, Nina," I said, and my voice cracked. I couldn't meet her eyes—could she see their torment from so far away, read my mind as well as she'd always been able to? "All I want is for you to be safe. We had a good run, but it's over."

I couldn't get out any more, because my throat had closed. I took a deep breath. "Save yourself. Please."

I couldn't read her face. It had been just weeks, but already, she looked more and more like a stranger.

There was a long, painful silence.

Nina's voice was low. "What happened to you, Reya?"

Each word was a punch to my gut, because each carried the enormity of my betrayal. I had dragged her out of a cave to cast her into deeper, darker recesses, and to her, that was heartbreaking.

"Nina, nothing happened to me," I insisted. "I'm still me. I still want the best for—"

Nina turned her back on me. "No," she snarled at Jahan, interrupting me mid-sentence. "No can do. I'm never joining you, *your Majesty*. So you can shove your deal up your—"

Devendra pounded his fist as the entire court erupted, but it could not be silenced. He looked beyond furious; he looked unhinged.

"Then you will never see the sun!" he screamed, before his voice was drowned out by howls and jeers. The soldiers converged on Nina, and my own servants stepped in front of me protectively, blocking me from view.

I caught sight of Nina before she was dragged away, no longer struggling. She looked up at me, eyes on fire, mouthing words I could barely hear: "Don't give up!"

She was being forced through the door, but I could see her dark head bobbing in and out of view as she turned back frantically towards me—"Do not let them break you!"

The doors slammed with a bone-jarring tremor, her voice still ringing in my head. Even as she called out to me, I knew deep down that it was too late. I had already been broken.

Seventeen

In every way that counted, I had failed her.

I couldn't stop thinking about Nina's eyes, deep and dark as dying embers. They seared my failure into my mind.

I could feel my failure permeating the *mahal*, as well. Nobles dropped their gaze when they saw me, their hands lingering uneasily at their swords. Through the library window, I watched blacksmiths cast bolts on all the gates, and soldiers line the minarets. It was almost as if Nina's final stand had threatened every semblance of peace left in the palace. There was no denying it—the Zakir crown was preparing for war.

The only person who seemed unaffected was Lady Sharati. She resumed my training with a vengeance, even though we hadn't received any messages from the king. While the Spider's curse did not prevent me from practicing magic under her watchful eye, I could feel it like a parasite in my veins, a constant omen of evil.

The fire flickered dimly as I paced my chambers, poring over the endless text of *Bhasa Pratana*. The runes seemed to blur before my eyes, but I was grateful for the distraction, even if I could never entirely escape what I had done.

Ink Soul lay open on the desk, inviting me to lose myself within its depths. But I could not indulge in it, at least not tonight. Because to write was to think, and to think was to feel. And to feel just wasn't an option.

Someone knocked on the door—too soft to be Naveen. "Kira?" I called, but there was no reply.

I had to stand on my tiptoes to reach the little peephole, but the darkened hallway was empty. My gaze dropped to my feet. At first, it was just my bare feet against the carpet. And there—so small I almost missed it—was a tiny purple envelope, jammed haphazardly beneath the door. I bent over and picked it up.

"Hello?"

My voice echoed in the hallway like a ghostly chorus—*hello? Hello? Hello?*

My fingers were shaking as I ripped the envelope apart. Inside, I found a card the size of my thumb, still warm with the sender's heat. The handwriting tugged at the back of my mind. For a moment, as I stared at the rounded edges, I thought I was looking at my own writing. But it couldn't have been—the grip was too tight, the lines too thin.

Written on the card's face were three words.

Bharata, take two.

I flipped it over.

Be ready.

I was aware of my heartbeat in my throat as I ripped

the note into shreds. Although the message was short, the meaning was clear. Enough of the Renegades had survived, and they were rallying for a second blow. Straight to the *mahal.*

Even as I closed my eyes, I could sense the door locked before me and the innumerable hallways wrapped around my chambers, and the massive gates around the *mahal,* and the palace hill, sprawling city, and Endless Jungle. We'd have to break through all of that to even have a fighting chance. It was going to be incredibly risky. All of us could die.

It occurred to me that we were all going to die anyway.

I jumped when I heard another knock, but this time, Naveen was standing in the doorway. "Are you okay?" he asked.

I blinked. "What?"

He laughed, but he couldn't hide his concern. I glanced at myself in the mirror and understood why—I looked pale, unspooled.

"I think so," I said, as casually as I could. "I don't want to practice magic tonight, though. Now's not the t—"

I stopped mid-sentence. Naveen's eyes were no longer on mine. They had fallen on the desk behind me. He was looking at *Ink Soul.*

"What's that?" he said.

I felt my stomach plunge.

"That's nothing—" I began, but before I could stop him, Naveen had crossed the room and picked up the book. I watched his eyes fly over the first page, the one about the kingdom over blue waters—the one I had never managed to finish.

Naveen looked at me, his eyes alight with an

expression I couldn't decipher. "Did you write this?" he asked at last.

I looked down. "Yes," I heard myself say. "But you can't tell anybody about it. It could be treasonous."

His brows furrowed. "I can see that. This is an act of rebellion."

I paced the room as Naveen turned the pages. His eyes travelled rapidly down the paragraphs and poems and fits and bursts of words, all the way until the end of the book.

"It's my *Ink Soul*," I told him, breaking the unbearable silence. "It's not much, but it keeps me sane. Writing helps me find myself. It…"

I trailed off, because *Ink Soul* felt so intimate, I couldn't imagine anyone else reading it, except maybe Nina. It wasn't so much a novel as it was a journey— one that was raw and honest, sometimes vile and unflattering. If it wasn't for the fact that Naveen had already seen me at my worst and saved me from myself, I would have ripped it from his hands.

> *"The girl carried a piece of a dead man's heart inside of her,"* Naveen read aloud. *"She was filled with scraps of wisdom gained from the spaces between his words—the moments when he wasn't trying to teach her anything except how to live."*

He set down the book. "That passage was about you," he said matter-of-factly. "The Bookweaver's daughter."

I stared at my feet. "Yeah, but I don't always get it," I said. "Look, even I don't understand my words sometimes. I'm not eloquent, not the way my father was—"

"I wasn't going to say that at all," said Naveen, surprising me. "You're good with words. Sometimes even incredible." He gave me a placating half-smile. "Why didn't you finish it, though?"

I shrugged, feeling painfully self-conscious. "Because my story isn't in my control anymore," I said at last. "Everything's changing too fast. You heard what I had to say to Nina at the trial. What we wanted, what we fought for— it can't happen."

I could see something in Naveen's eyes, and it gutted me. I'd seen him laughing, snarling, smiling, and I'd think I knew him, but occasionally he'd do something that suggested another universe locked away inside of him. I'd seen glimpses of that universe before—when he talked about Kira. When he took my hand and anchored me. And now again, as his fingers tapped the cover of *Ink Soul.*

"Say something," I begged.

He pulled a hand through his vivid brown hair, looking more tired than I'd ever seen him.

"I wish things could be better," Naveen said finally. "Whenever I talk to you, I see an entire world that could be better. And then I remember that I work for the Zakir dynasty, and the fantasy pops like a bubble."

I couldn't meet his eyes.

"Why don't you do something, then?" I asked. "You're a Mage. You're on the inside. You have a chance to change things for the better."

I didn't mean to sound accusatory, but Naveen's face fell. "Because of Kira," he said, and he said it like an apology. "Because when I'm silent, Kira is safe."

As much as I wanted to deny it, I understood. Wasn't that exactly why I was sitting here, learning to perform *vayati,* prepared to let the world burn as long as Nina survived unscathed?

"In another life, we could have been friends," I said, after a long pause. "Actual friends. We might've learned magic together from a guru. We would've grown into Mages, and I would've been the Bookweaver."

"You could've finished your book," said Naveen wistfully. "Kira could become a healer."

"Nina would be an architect," I added quietly. "My father would be alive, and so would my mother and my grandparents and the entire city of Bharata. God, I—" I was annoyed to feel tears in my eyes.

"Do you believe in fate?" he asked me, dutifully looking away until my eyes were dry. I frowned at him, and he said, "Not that our futures are dictated by the ancestors or ruled by *karma* or mapped out in the stars, not any of that. But that everything happens for a reason."

"No," I said automatically. "No. If that were true, none of us would be in so much pain. There could be no reason for it."

"No?" echoed Naveen. "Because the way I see it, there's usually a thousand layers to every moment we live, every decision we make. And while we can't discern every layer or how it overlaps with the rest of the world, it's comforting to know there's a common reason to all of our experiences, that we're not all just shouting into chasms."

He said this all in one run-on breath, like he was afraid I would stop him.

I didn't, because I had seen it again—that unexpected glimpse of his universe. And for the first time, I viewed the world through Naveen Chadav's eyes.

I imagined being on the winning side of things and finding myself among strangers. I imagined looking around and realizing that I was incompatible with everything I thought I knew, the only exception to my own beliefs. And I thought that maybe I understood his need to find reason in the conflict that was his life.

"Maybe you're right," I said. "But I can't let myself believe in anything greater than myself. Because then I can't own my guilt and pain. I can't hold myself accountable for everything I've done."

Naveen's eyes were too sympathetic. "You don't have to constantly punish yourself, Reya," he said. "You can believe in your purpose and forgive yourself. You can—"

"Naveen," I interrupted. My pulse pounded wildly as I tugged *Ink Soul* away from him. "What I hope you never have to understand is the raw, living guilt of having ruined lives."

I took a breath. "I am so irredeemable that I cannot be a part of your greater purpose. I'd ruin it."

I could tell he was longing to cut across, but I ignored him.

"Here's how it really works," I said. "There's no reason for anything that happens in this awful, miserable universe. But we all have a choice. We can make something beautiful out of it, or we can set it all on fire. We all have a choice, and mine has been to burn down everything in my path, every time, without fail."

Without realizing it, I'd shredded the corner of my shirt, and the lace was unraveling in my fingers. I couldn't meet his eyes.

Naveen sighed. "Reya, you're not irredeemable," he said. "Nobody is."

"Then you don't know me," I said, with more cold-ness than I'd intended.

He looked a little shocked, and the sight of his face brought the words to my lips. Before I could stop myself, I had seized his arm, startling him.

"Listen, Naveen." The words tumbled out in a rush. "You've been a good friend, so I am going to warn you now—take Kira and leave the *mahal* tonight. I can't tell you any more than that, but you need to get out safely."

Naveen frowned, but did not remove his arm from my grip. "What are you talking about?" he said. "Reya, why should I—"

My fury was back—an ember glowing in the back of my mind. "Because I cannot be responsible for your pain!" I said. "You and Kira have shown nothing but kindness to me. I'm trying to repay the favor here and save your life."

All I could think about was my anger: anger against everyone who had ever cared for me, loved me, offered me a kind word. Every one of the suicidal Renegades, Nina included, who were prepared to put everything on the line again—to die for me, *again.* Anger against Naveen, who couldn't get his head out of his perfect purposeful universe to see me as the killer I was.

"Reya," Naveen was saying. "If something danger-ous is happening soon, how will you protect yourself? Why are you so bent on letting yourself burn?"

I shoved Naveen away.

As he staggered back, I said in one angry breath, "Naveen, you have everything I don't have. You have family and freedom and hope for a future. Do not drag yourself into all of my pain. Do not try to fight an enemy you barely understand. Do not make the same mistakes I did."

My voice broke as I ran out of air. With all the certainty I could muster, I added, "We all have a choice. And my choice is to save your life."

Naveen looked like he wanted to argue, but he hesitated. Without another word, he walked away, slamming the door a little too hard behind him. The lock crashed into place with a rattle I felt in my bones.

Ink Soul Chapter VIII

The pearl reminded me of a teardrop the day my father gave it to me.

"What is it, Father?" I said, running my fingers over it. It was small enough to conceal in a child's palm, not perfectly spherical yet—it would take seven years of nervous rubbing until it assumed the roundness it had the day it cracked. "It looks like a beetle egg. Or a sad lady's tears."

"It's a pearl, Reya," my father told me. "Do you know what a pearl is?"

"Yes. This," I answered, and my father laughed, tousling my soft brown hair. "Wait until you grow up," he said. "You'll make Kasmira's wittiest sages shake in fear."

"No," I countered. "When I'm grown up, I'll be just like you. I'll be a Bookweaver."

I was too young to register the agony that flashed across my father's face, although perhaps he hid it well. "Reya," he said quietly, "you know you're not supposed to say that. It's a secret."

"A secret," I repeated. It was an exciting word, full of mystery, reminding me of days spent reading past my bedtime, hidden under the covers so my mother wouldn't see. It felt like sneaking into the kitchen when my father's back was turned and swiping mangoes off the table. Just when I thought I'd gotten away, he'd whirl around and sweep me up, tickling me until I confessed. He'd peel the mangoes and we'd eat them together. They were delicious, juicy secrets.

My father staggered back suddenly, and I felt the pearl burn hot in my hand. I dropped it with a clatter. "It just hurt me—"

He bent over to retrieve the pearl, but I could tell from the stoop of his shoulders that he was in pain. "That's because it's special," he told me. "If it gets hot like that, it means that I'm not feeling well. And I might need your help."

"I'll always help you," I told him, and something flickered behind his eyes.

"Thank you, Reya," he said. "Now tell me, what's your new name?"

"Reya Patel," I said. "Not Reya Kandhari. Because that's a secret."

"Good," said my father. His smile sent warmth flooding through my body. "Are you ready for your new life?"

I nodded, and together, we slipped out of the hut and walked until we were standing in front of a pair of huge iron gates, locked beneath a royal sign. Between its bars, I could see endless golden stalks, mango trees, cows.

"Fields," I read aloud. "Is this the place?"

My father leaned against his crutches, breathing hard. "Yes," he answered, but it sounded more like a wheeze. He gave me a kiss across the forehead, clutching his staffs for support.

"Go on, now," he said. "I'll watch from here. They don't let fathers with crutches come into the Fields."

I ran through the gates, ignoring the scowls of the overlords I had not yet learned to fear. I ran through the golden grass and crowds of peasants until I collided with a raven-haired girl.

"Why are you smiling?" she demanded. She tossed her long hair impressively, and I gazed up at her in wonder. "Because today is my first day," I told her. "I'm Reya Patel."

"I'm Nina Nadeer," the girl said. "And you shouldn't be smiling. If you look like you have extra energy, they give you extra work."

"Why should I listen to you?" I countered, hands on my hips. The girl frowned. "Because I'm nine, and you're not," she said decisively. "I'll take care of you from now on, if you want."

I opened my mouth to say that there was no need—I already had somebody to take care of me. But when I turned back, the Field gates were empty. My father had gone.

"Your father's not coming back," said Nina matter-of-factly. "Mine didn't. He dropped me here when I was a little girl and never came back. I think that gate does something to fathers. It makes them stop loving their babies."

"My father isn't like that," I reassured Nina, but as I gazed back at the empty gates, I wasn't so sure.

The dawn sky was streaked with shadows when Sita and Trisha drew the curtains the next morning. My eyes stung and blurred—I'd barely slept during the night, heart pounding over what the morning would bring.

To my relief, Kira was nowhere to be seen, which could only mean one thing: Naveen had heeded my advice and taken her to safety.

I smiled at Sita and Trisha as they filled my bath. "Why don't you both take today off?" I asked, trying to sound casual. "I can take care of myself this morning."

Sita frowned. "Are you sure, my lady?"

"Very sure," I said forcefully. "Go to the bazaar today. The weather's lovely."

The sky outside had turned an ashy gray, but Sita said nothing. She and Trisha merely nodded and slipped through the door, closing it much more gently than Naveen had.

Lady Sharati appraised me coldly in the library after breakfast. "I don't suppose you know where the Chadav boy's run off to," she said briskly. "He didn't submit his report last night."

"No," I squeaked, and she sighed. Devendra, however, narrowed his eyes.

"Certain you don't know where he is, Kandhari?" he said quietly. "Looked to me like the two of you were getting close."

"Really," I said, forcing my voice to sound emotionless, like Devendra's. "If I didn't know better, I'd say you were getting jealous."

Devendra opened his mouth to retort, but was silenced by Sharati. "Chadav's absence aside," she said, "the time to perform *vayati* approaches, and you must be prepared. Today, we will refine your Ancient Kasmiri vocabulary."

She glared at me. "You aren't listening."

I blinked and pushed my hair out of my eyes. Maybe I was imagining it, but I could have sworn I'd seen a hulking figure crouched behind the bookshelf—

Noting my gaze, Devendra turned and peered behind him. "What are you looking at?" he demanded.

"Nothing," I said, but color had flooded my cheeks. I could feel Devendra's hawk-like gaze on me.

"Something's not right," he said slowly. "You're hiding something. You're nervous."

"And you're losing your grip," I argued, but Devendra's stare felt like a weight.

"Kandhari," he said slowly. "If there's anything you're hiding…" His voice trailed off dangerously.

I was spared a reply, because right above Sharati's head, the shelves began to sway. Every tome and scroll began to thrum ominously. A single book fell from the shelf, narrowly missing Devendra's head. He whirled around.

"What the—"

And then the bookshelf smashed in half.

As shards flew everywhere, sending clouds of dust flying, I saw a man step out of the smoky gloom, his voice colored with dry amusement. "Nice to see you, too," Niam said.

Eighteen

For a moment, he was a shadowy silhouette on top of the broken bookshelf. Then Niam rolled to his feet in a blur of speed, weaving through the bookshelves like he was more liquid than solid. Devendra drew his sword, looking murderous.

There was a shout behind me.

"Halt!"

A squadron of soldiers burst through the opposite door, and Lady Sharati flagged them down frantically. "The intruder!" she said. "He's run that way—"

Rough hands seized the back of my arms.

I spun around, nearly colliding with the soldier who had seized me from behind. Instinct took over, and I kicked wildly, but the soldier dodged my flailing limbs and hoisted me into the air. Somehow, I managed to smash aside the soldier's mask—and froze, mid-punch. The face beneath belonged to Aisha Chori.

These weren't soldiers. These were Renegades.

"Stop fighting me, damn it," she hissed. "We're trying to rescue you—"

Just then, a dozen actual soldiers poured in through the doors, weapons aloft. "Pursue the intruder!" one shouted to Aisha, evidently mistaking her for his comrade.

Aisha didn't wait for further orders. She turned and ran, seizing me by the arm. The Renegades formed a protective huddle around me as we thundered through the caved-in door.

"Wait!"

I turned in a panic to see Lady Sharati at my heels, her veil askew. Bolts of magic levitated above her palms. "Where do you think you're going?"

Her golden eyes met mine briefly before landing on Aisha, whose guilty expression was as good as a giveaway. An inkling of the truth dawned on Sharati's face.

I raised my arms defensively, but there was no hope of stopping her as she opened her mouth and screamed, "*Inimico!*"

And the room erupted.

I felt myself flying backwards, uncontrollably fast. Before I could stop myself, I'd smashed into a bookshelf. A deluge of tomes poured on my head—tiny lights burst before my eyes. Everyone within a ten-foot radius was blasted by Sharati's spell—friend and foe alike. Aisha stumbled—Aran pulled her out of Sharati's range, slicing through a row of books as he did so.

It was a mark of the gravity of the situation that I could not object to the destruction of literature.

Sharati's mouth was opening again—to scream a second curse, to shout for the soldiers? We never found out, because before she could gather her voice, I jumped onto her back, completely forgetting for a wild instant that she was a fully trained Mage. Sharati bucked violently, but I clung to her bony shoulders. That was all Aisha needed.

"*Inimi*—"

Aisha smashed Sharati across the jaw, cutting her spell short. Sharati crumpled beneath a broken table and was still.

The shelves were starting to sway precariously, chunks of wood raining down like hail. We needed no further invitation to leave. I stumbled to my feet, hitched up my skirt, and ran towards the door.

Right before Aisha flung me into the hallway, I caught a glimpse of the war raging inside the library— manuscripts in shreds, dust everywhere, Devendra's sword a blur of silver in the air. Niam ducked, laughing like he was having the time of his life, even as the blade whistled past his head—

"Devendra!" I shouted. "Missing someone?"

I saw him whip around.

The prince's eyes widened and he lunged, but he was too late—Niam slipped out from behind him and through the doorway. I slammed the door shut as Devendra hurled his sword at us—it hit the doorframe with a deadly twang.

"Move on," Niam urged. "They're coming—"

A second later, the library door burst open once more. I flung myself behind a column as five imperial soldiers hurtled after Aisha; she twisted around a corner, leading them out of sight. Niam dispatched two soldiers with a powerful kick, sending them tumbling.

"Are you hurt?" I called, catching up to him.

I could see the thrill of battle on Niam's face; it made his eyes wild, cheeks ruddy.

"No, but we're outnumbered," he said. "We've got to find a way out of this godforsaken place—"

The soldier beneath him was beginning to stir. "Don't watch," Niam warned me. He lifted his sword and smashed its hilt into the soldier's head, knocking him out with a crunch that made my insides twist. He saw my expression and sighed. "I told you not to watch."

"I'm fine," I said, even though I wasn't.

The shouts and clanging swords were getting closer, and Niam's jaw tightened in grim resolve. "Are you up for a fight?" he asked.

"Always," I replied, and he laughed.

"That's good, Bookweaver, because that's what we're about to get."

Niam handed me a sword, and I couldn't help but remember the time he had handed me his blade in Bharata. This time, the sword felt light in my arms. I had gotten stronger.

I could truly appreciate how massive the *mahal* was now that we were breaking our way out. The identical hallways warped and merged into an endless maze of columns, distinguished only by the ever-growing piles of fallen fighters.

"Here," I panted, pulling Niam into a hall I recognized. "Come on, there's a courtyard this way—"

The door across from us swung open, and a horde of soldiers burst into the room, led by Devendra Zakir. He was limping, but his expression was livid.

"KANDHARI!"

Devendra let out my name with a terrible bull-roar

of fury, and I dove out of the way. Swords smashed across the room, filling the air with metallic screams.

Niam stepped in front of me, but Devendra knocked him aside, his sword pointing straight at my heart. I twisted away and tore along the corridor, torrents of glass splintering like rain.

I could hear Devendra gaining on me, his ragged breathing growing louder even as the sounds of battle grew softer. I hung a wild left—he stumbled but kept on coming, wounded leg and all—

The floor beneath me gave way to reveal a spiral staircase, twisted like the belly of a serpent.

And then I was falling down stone step after stone step, legs wheeling uncontrollably, jarring against the banisters until I collapsed onto the landing. My sword skittered across the floor.

Devendra staggered down the steps, his leg dragging awkwardly. I wheeled around, but I was trapped.

"Zakir," I said desperately, but he cut across.

"Why?" he shouted, his voice echoing in the close quarters. "Why do you constantly defy me? You have *everything*. You have a mission from his Majesty himself. You have—"

"Because I don't want it!" I interrupted, because I knew it would incense him. "Because you can't bring back my murdered father. Because you want to murder my friends. Maybe you put power before the people you care about, but I don't."

His purple eyes were like a seer's amethysts: twin omens of pain and death.

"The crazy, suicidal stunts you pull, like this home invasion?" he said, advancing slowly towards me. "It's like you have a death wish."

"Maybe I do," I snapped, surprising myself. Devendra hadn't taken his eyes off of mine; he wasn't looking at Niam's sword, laying on the floor beside my feet. If he came close enough...

"If there's one thing I learned from my father," Devendra said quietly, "there's no honor in dying for a lost cause. Now come with me before I—"

"Yeah, I don't think so," I said.

With all the strength I had left, I dove at the sword—it thrummed in my grasp, the leather still warm, and I slashed at Devendra, taking him by surprise. His arms flailed as he tried to keep his balance, but I kicked savagely at his wounded leg—

The crown prince tumbled to the floor, but not before he grabbed the hem of my wildly impractical *sari*, jerking me forward. The ground rushed up at me. Devendra stumbled to his feet, but I grabbed his leg. He screamed, a guttural sound that made me shiver—

Somehow, I was on top of him, and I raised the sword and brought it down...

The blade bent.

The arrested momentum caused the sword to jerk to one side, twisting my wrist with it. Swearing, I staggered back, struggling to make sense of what had happened.

A haze of bright magical heat burst from Devendra— too sharp to be mine, too icy. I saw his eyes, reflected on the steel of my blade, widen in fear. And that's when I understood.

Devendra had used magic.

I scrabbled backwards, sword forgotten on the floor, but Devendra couldn't seem to move. The magic was swirling around him, glowing and potent.

"You're a Mage?" I said, and the sound of my voice seemed to jerk him from his stupor.

But Devendra, a Mage? No, the heir of the anti-magic Zakir dynasty couldn't be a sorcerer, he just couldn't—but there he was, spasming with magic and panic combined. Devendra was clawing his way towards me, arms outstretched—

His lips moved to form my name, and I leapt to my feet. He was still convulsing when I rushed up the stairs and turned the corner, just as another girl rounded it from the other side.

I grabbed the wall to slow myself down, but even so, I crashed into her. She let out a familiar shriek, shaking dark hair from her eyes, and my heart leapt.

"Nina!"

"Reya!" Nina gave me a smothering hug; half of her face was purple, but just like Niam in the library, she was smiling from ear to ear. "Quite a reunion, don't you think?"

"Nina," I repeated breathlessly, too overwhelmed to say anything else, drinking in her aliveness, her whole-ness—"Where is everyone?"

She shrugged helplessly. "We all got split up," she said. "There are more soldiers than the Renegades were prepared for. Niam thinks they must have suspected we were coming."

"They did? But how?"

Her face mirrored my confusion, but a pit had formed in my stomach. I had only warned one person in the palace that the Renegades were coming.

"It doesn't matter," Nina was saying. "We can still get out of here. Come on—"

She stopped mid-sentence as guards flooded one

end of the hallway. I tugged her back into a stone recess, but they had already noticed us. Nina took my hand as the soldiers converged. "Run!" she screamed.

I didn't need to be told twice. We dashed down the hall, Nina's sword swinging to the rhythm of her feet.

In spite of everything, it felt like nothing had changed as we ran, hand in hand, from death itself—the soldiers gave chase as we tore down the stairs, jumping the last couple of steps. Nina slammed another door behind us—

A metallic hand forced it back open.

And like a bad nightmare, the temperature was dropping, the doorknob frosting over with ice—

"You thought you could escape without my notice?" a cold voice chuckled, terrible as rocks scraping bone. "*I see all*, Bookweaver. And although I alerted the soldiers to take care of your cohorts, I decided that I would look after you myself."

As the Spider advanced, the hallway seemed to darken, blotting out the mid-morning sun. Its silver mouth was smiling, and Nina was shivering beside me. As I raised my hands and stoked the fire within myself, I had Nina in mind, not the consequences.

"*Temperus!*" I screamed, but the flames didn't come.

Instead, the Spider's curse erupted from my very soul.

My mother was screaming, beating at my father's chest. Her eyes were open graves. The venom in her gaze ripped me open, ensnaring my insides, reaching for my pulsating, throbbing heart.

I screwed my eyes shut against the agony within, but the Spider's curse was slicing through me with a vengeance, and I fell to the floor—

"Reya!" Nina shrieked as the Spider reached for her, but I could barely hear her. I could already see her body—*still and lifeless and cold, her black hair spilling like blood*—as pain pinched the edges of my vision.

The real Nina was slashing with her sword, but with a snap of the Spider's fingers, the blade flew out of her grasp and across the room.

Exhausted, I staggered towards her, ignoring the fact that my nerves were splitting, that the Spider was a good ten yards ahead of me, that we were both about to die.

I reached her just as the Spider lifted its arms. I could see the end, but my breath was surprisingly even.

My body would be her shield, just as Nina had shielded me many times before. My eyes glanced around—not for a way out, but for something beautiful to look at, to give me strength for the coming moment.

Right before the Spider's metal body touched mine, I focused on the stormy gray of Nina's eyes.

"*Reya!*"

I opened my eyes, and my heart quaked as I saw Naveen.

Naveen's hands opened, and water rose like a column of molten glass. He was expressionless, but a terrible fury roiled in the back of his eyes as he released all his power at once, taking the Spider by surprise and knocking it to the floor.

"Get out of here!" I gasped. I leaned against the wall and felt myself sliding down, knees buckled uselessly beneath me. "Naveen, there are more soldiers coming …"

"We all have a choice," he told me, his voice strangely steady. It was the last thing he said to me.

His head blurred out of focus. My mouth shaped his name uselessly as I passed out, water flowing like blood.

Nineteen

After that night, the *mahal* was quiet. It was a painful, icy silence, like a final prayer.

Devendra visited me shortly after I was locked back in my chambers. His face was white as he stalked towards me. His long legs crossed the room in two strides, so I didn't have enough time to pretend I was asleep. "Kandhari," he said.

I ignored him.

"Reya," he said, taking me by surprise. He'd never called me by my name before. I turned around.

"Here to gloat?" I croaked, my voice cracking from disuse. "Save it."

The prince looked terrible. His angular cheekbones, normally handsome, made him look sick, skull-like.

"That's not why I'm here," Devendra said. "Look. What you think you saw there today—"

"Are you referring to that delightfully illegal magic trick? I wonder what Daddy's going to think about that."

His eyes flashed dangerously. For the first time, Devendra looked terrified, and I knew how much his father's honor meant to him. If Jahan found out that his son was one of the very Mages he so hated, Devendra would be crushed.

"That wasn't magic—" he started angrily.

"Please," I interrupted coldly. "I know magic when I see it. How long have you known?"

He recoiled. "I didn't," he insisted. "I don't know how it happened. I can't be a Mage."

I smirked, a little, in spite of everything.

"Welcome to the club," I said. "If we find enough members, maybe we can spring for matching turbans."

Devendra reddened. "This isn't a joke," he said. "You have no idea what's at stake. This is bigger than you. This is bigger than anything you could ever imagine—"

"No, *you* have no idea what's at stake," I snapped. "What your father wants me to do—it's not right. Magic isn't supposed to be abused like that. It will destroy whatever balance this kingdom has ever known."

Devendra pulled himself to his full height.

"I am the imperial commander of Kasmira, damn it," he shouted. "You won't tell anyone what you saw, or I will—"

"Kill me?" I finished, tears rising to my eyes. But this time, they weren't tears of grief. A strangled chuckle escaped me, then another, until I had burst into laughter—maniacal, desperate, end-of-the-world laughter.

"Oh, Devendra," I choked out. "I'm already dead."

Now, hours or possibly days later, the smile had faded from my face. I eventually noticed *Ink Soul* had disappeared from my desk, which could only mean that Sharati had confiscated my traitorous manuscript, taking with her my only lifeline within these walls.

I should have been nervous, but the missing *Ink Soul* was the least of my worries. In spite of everything that had happened, what I regretted most was that my room had no clock. Without it, it was impossible to tell how much time had passed. The faint cracks of light from the shuttered windows had stretched and bent like wax, leading me to think the sun had risen multiple times over, but I couldn't be sure.

Someone had been sliding meals through a slot in my door.

The slot opened again, jerking me from my thoughts. There was a scraping noise as a bowl of *korma* slid through, followed by two bits of *naan* bread, one of which fell off the tray.

In three lunges, I crossed the room and struck the door so hard that the hinges rattled.

"Wait!" I screamed, my voice rusty. "What time is it?"

There was no answer.

I stood up and slammed my hand against the door. "Get back here!"

The lock clicked, and the door opened at last. I looked up to see Lady Sharati, her nose slightly wrinkled at the stench. There was a faded bruise across her chin from where Aisha had punched her. "You can stop screaming now," she said.

I tried to summon anger, but I couldn't. I had been so starved for information that even Sharati's annoyed face was almost welcome.

"Calm down," she ordered. "We have a lot of work to do."

"Lady Sharati," I said, before she could leave. "What—what time is it?"

The Mage regarded me for a moment. "It's noon," she replied at last. "It's been two days."

At the sound of her bell, Sita and Trisha entered the room. My breath caught in my throat. "Where's Kira?" I asked. The two girls wouldn't look at me as they set to work brushing out my hair.

"Tell me," I repeated, my voice deadly calm, before it broke into a shout: "*Where is she?*"

Trisha gave a start and dropped the hairbrush. "Kira Chadav has been taken, miss," Sita whispered. "They're questioning her because of her brother."

Because of Naveen. Because of me.

All I could think about was the kindness Kira had shown me during my first weeks in the palace: bringing me tea, defending me, slipping me encouragement. She and Naveen were the first friends I'd had since Nina. And now she was in danger.

I thought bathing would make me feel better. I was wrong. The leftover scrapes from the fight stung fiercely in the water, and my servants were no help: Trisha seemed perpetually on the verge of tears, while Sita stared determinedly away, tossing a towel haphazardly in my direction.

We had almost built a relationship. Now they hated me. The thing was, I didn't blame them.

The library reminded me of an open wound.

The dust had been swept hastily to one side of the room, the broken shelves piled precariously like bones. I tried not to think about how empty the place felt without Naveen's reassuring presence beside mine.

For the next half hour, Lady Sharati didn't stop pacing.

"It's time to prepare to perform *vayati*," Sharati said. "Tomorrow, there will be a massive ceremony held in the throne room. His majesty has invited nobles from all over Kasmira to attend. It will be the pinnacle of his reign."

She cleared her throat, enunciating every word. "Your *vayati* must be perfect. We will draft the spell today. And tomorrow, you will weave the final lines in the presence of Jahan, thus bringing it to life."

I felt sickened. Writing the final line was like sealing the fate.

"There are three requirements for *vayati*," I reminded her. "It can't be for my benefit, it has to be in Ancient Kasmiri, and I have to unlock my Yogi state."

"Indeed," said Sharati. "You'll notice we're a little short on Ancient Kasmiri translators, so you'll be needing this." She pulled out the massive copy of *Bhasa Pratana*. I had a fleeting memory of Naveen holding the book with reverence, and my mouth felt dry.

Sharati opened the sprawling pages of Runic Code. "All right," I said, as though I wrote monumental stories in an extinct language every day. "And the Yogi state?"

"It cannot be forcibly induced," admitted Sharati. "Your training thus far will give you the stamina you need to maintain the state. And as for awakening it— well, his Majesty has no shortage of ways to persuade you to do so."

Naveen. Nina. Kira. Fear prickled in my chest. I took a deep breath. "Let's begin, then," I said.

I raised my pen to the parchment.

He was immortal.

The scratch of nib on parchment reminded me of sword against stone, against metal, against flesh. I closed my eyes against the memories, tucking them into the back of my mind. There would be no more bloodshed, not after this.

His glory threw the rays of the sun into despair.
King Jahan Zakir had the entire world at his feet.

My throat constricted as the words poured out of my pen. Each letter seemed to hurt as it formed.

I couldn't shake the awful feeling that I was dooming my kingdom.

Farkandh, Kampi, and Indira fell like crushed sap-
lings, one by one. Blood lapped the king's feet—blood of
the enemies—their final tributes to their rightful master.

Ragged scraps of words sailed through my brain, but they did not sing to me like they usually did. Instead they throbbed, each word marching painfully and reluctantly through my wrist, into the pen, and onto the parchment.

Sharati helped me decide on the final sentence to complete the spell. "It has to be perfect," she warned me.

For the immortal leader was Jahan Zakir,
who would lead Kasmira into a golden age that
the bards would sing of for ages to come.

I hated every word.

The words linked together and flowed like water, poetic and radiant. But there was no pretending: I knew that when woven, translated into Ancient Kasmiri, and fused with magic, they could bring down kingdoms that had stood unwavering since the beginning of time.

I thought, for a moment, about my missing *Ink Soul*. More than anything, I wanted the words of my father for comfort. My father, who had taught me to love words before he taught me to weave them. My father, who left too soon and left an enormous legacy behind him. My father, who would be heartbroken to see what had befallen the kingdom he loved.

At last, Sharati nodded. "This will do," she said. There was a pause in which we sized each other up. As I stared into her cat-like eyes, I tried to summon my usual rage against the cruel woman who had been the face of my anger for the past months, but I found nothing. Because Sharati, like me, was just a pawn. And we were both playing Jahan's game.

"It's nearly midnight," Lady Sharati noted. She was right: the candles had dripped down to greasy stubs, and the shadows had sunk low. "You'd better rest. You'll need your full strength for tomorrow."

Exhausted, I followed her to my quarters. For a fleeting moment, I imagined jumping on her back again, throwing her to the floor, and making another run for it. But the idea disappeared as quickly as it came. There was nowhere left to run, anyway.

"Good night, Bookweaver," said Sharati, surprising me. It was the first time she'd ever said something remotely kind. Before she could lock the door, I turned around.

"Wait," I said. "You're a Mage, too. You're going to suffer if my *vayati* works. What do you get out of it?"

Her eyes were blank, or perhaps it was just the torchlight reflected in them.

"Honor and pride in serving my kingdom," she said at last. "What his Majesty represents is greater than you. It's greater than me. It's something the thugs you kept company with could never understand."

She finally broke eye contact as she locked the door behind her. "And tomorrow, you will serve your kingdom as well."

My father visited me in my dreams that night.

In my sleep, the Bookweaver was not the proud, laughing man I chose to remember him as. That night he was his hunched, crippled self, eyebrows furrowed in despair.

"Father?" I said. He looked at me, and his lips turned down in disappointment.

"What's wrong?" I pressed.

"What's wrong?" he repeated. He sounded brittle, disbelieving. "Reya, everything is wrong. You let me die. And now you're helping the one who killed me become a thousand times stronger."

I bit my lip. "Father, I—"

"I know you think you have no way out," he continued. "But what did your mother always teach you?"

"There's always a way out if you're persistent enough to find it," I chanted obediently along with him. His voice sounded like mine, but our voices echoed, clashing with strange discordance. It made the

hairs stand up on the back of my neck.

"I know that. But you don't understand—" I began.

"It doesn't matter," he said dismissively. "You have a second chance to repair everything. You can save me." As he spoke, he opened his palm. Resting inside it was another pearl, gleaming faintly with what I now recognized to be magic.

"A second chance," I echoed quietly.

My father looped a thread around the pearl with the deft fingers of a writer, forming a necklace. "May I?" he asked, moving to fasten it at my throat. My head started to nod automatically, but the words wouldn't come.

The pearl was still sitting in his palm. For a moment, I was seized with the urge to take it, to tie it around my neck, be the daughter from the Fringes once more. That was who I was: the daughter who tended mango trees as she tended for her own father, sweet and self-less and good.

But I was also the daughter who resented her own father. I was the daughter who led soldiers to the Bookweaver's front door. I was the daughter who was about to burn his legacy into ashes.

"No," I said. "You may not."

The Bookweaver looked like I'd slapped him. "What?"

"I am about to change my life," I said. "And I will not be burdened by you again. I am taking this journey alone."

The pain was palpable in his eyes. "I never wanted to burden you, Reya," he insisted. "And I'm so sorry you felt that way. All I wanted was to guide you."

"Guide me?" I repeated angrily. "You didn't teach me a damn thing. You left me in the dark about every-thing that mattered. You left me alone."

"That was for your own protection." He was pleading with me. "I didn't want to lead you into the murk of my world. You had enough darkness of your own."

"Well, that was a mistake," I said in a tight little voice I could scarcely recognize. "I'm not someone you'd be proud of. I used to be glad you were gone, so you wouldn't see who I'd become."

My father opened his mouth to protest, but I couldn't be stopped, not now.

"I'm not going to follow your path," I said. "I'm going to follow Jahan's path. You know why?" I spat the next words out with a bitterness I didn't know I could muster. "Because I'm not the Bookweaver's daughter. Not anymore."

My voice rang in the air, burning bridges, building walls between us.

My father sighed. "Well, I hope you can find her within you again," he said quietly. He looked at his palm, and the pearl disappeared with a whisper of magic. "And I never wanted you to follow my path, or anyone else's, for that matter. I always knew you would pave your own."

With that, he turned on his heel and walked away into the darkness of deep sleep, leaving a second unsaid goodbye in his wake.

Twenty

It felt like I'd barely closed my eyes before a frantic Sharati was shaking me awake, and Trisha and Sita were herding me in front of the mirror, their fingers trembling as they laced me into a regal purple *sari*.

When I closed the chamber door behind me, the lock clicked shut with a sense of finality. I think I knew, then, that I wasn't coming back.

The sun still hadn't risen when we reached the doors that guarded the throne room. There was only the briefest moment to steel my nerves before they swung open.

The throne room was so vast it made the mirrored Council look like a closet. Adorned with tapestries of bloody hunts and purple velvet, giant portraits of ancient royalty lined the hallway. And at the very end of the hall, sitting so still that I nearly mistook him for a portrait himself, was King Jahan Zakir.

He was reading a book bound in leather the color

of deep wine, or perhaps blood. He lifted a slender finger, as if to say, *"Give me a moment."* Over the top of the book, his eyes brushed mine, and I felt a jolt of electricity pass through me. The room seemed to have started spinning.

I guess I had been expecting the devil himself on the throne. But somehow, Jahan was even worse, because he was the devil with a beguilingly human face. I could see the resemblance to his son immediately in his eyes. They were clever, sharp purple orbs, gleaming unusually bright for the small man who owned them.

He set down his book and raised his hand. The lords assembled in the chamber and bowed—even the Spider kept a reverent distance. Only Devendra, sulking at his side, continued to gaze resolutely away.

"Welcome, Bookweaver," said Jahan. "It's my pleasure to finally meet you."

"If only it was under different circumstances," I said.

I heard Sharati gasp, but Jahan merely smiled. It was a thin, lipless snake-smile that didn't quite reach his eyes.

"I understand," he said. "Your anger still boils. I know your type, Bookweaver, because I see it in myself. Those of us in power must learn to hide our emotions behind a mask, as I'm sure you're learning."

I barely dared to breathe as he continued.

"It may surprise you to learn that I admire you," he said quietly. "You and I have both come from darker beginnings. We're the underdogs. We had to fight for what we believed in. Nothing was ever handed to us."

"Then why are you doing this?" I heard myself say. "Why are you tormenting your citizens and persecuting Mages?"

Jahan granted me a fleeting smile. "They told me that you like stories," he said amicably. "Well, this one is mine."

Without waiting for my response, he slipped off his throne and started down the steps.

"My brother, Viraj, was an imbecile. He thought that power could be shared—among the Yogis, among the Mages, among the peasantry. He inherited his power, so he never knew the valor of fighting for glory. I, meanwhile, was the second son. I was powerless, so I could see it all with clear eyes."

Everything was silent except for the Spider's ragged breaths. Jahan lowered his voice, turning his gaze squarely upon me.

"They say that power should only be given to those with no desire for it," he said musingly. "But you and I both know that's untrue. Power belongs to those who take it, not those Mages to whom it's handed upon birth. That knowledge made me a symbol for those who believed in me."

He smiled.

"And so I, like you, rose up. I took back my throne for what I knew to be true—that power is worthless unless sanctified by honor. And yes, people had to die, but they were a necessary sacrifice for the greater good."

There was a theatrical pause before he delivered the punchline.

"Truly, Bookweaver, what makes me any different than you?"

In that horrible moment, I realized he was right.

I had blood on my hands, thick and red as that on Jahan's. I had single-handedly destroyed the entire city of Bharata, raising fire and pain. I was responsible for

unthinkable pain, all in service of a greater ideal I
never quite attained. At the end of the day, how was I
any better than Jahan?

King Jahan slowly descended into the hall. His gait
was oddly distorted—half-limp, half-glide. As he
spoke, his voice rose to a fever pitch.

"We are one and the same, Bookweaver! Join me,
and together we can weave the kingdom that we
always dreamed of."

I stared into his purple eyes, and all I wanted was
to believe him.

"But—" I started.

"But what?" interrupted Jahan. "You will eradicate
the remaining rebels and Mages—the weeds that threat-
en the flowerbed of Kasmira. *That* is your destiny."

"They're not weeds," someone muttered.

Jahan whirled around to face Devendra, his head
bowed, standing beside him.

"What did you say, son?" said the king, his voice
deadly soft.

Devendra's face had turned white.

I used to think that Devendra was terrifying, but I
suddenly realized that it had always been the other
way around. Devendra was the one who was constantly terrified. And his worst fear was his father.

"Speak up!" Jahan snarled. "If you're going to interrupt your king's ceremony, at least be a man about it
and raise your voice!"

Devendra finally looked Jahan in the eye, and
when he spoke, his voice was steady. "I said, Mages
aren't weeds."

His father gave a sharp bark of laughter, but his eyes
were narrowed. "Has your time hunting the Bookweaver

caused you to go soft, son?" he asked. "Of course they're weeds. They ensnarl the foundation of Kasmira, causing all around them to wilt and die."

The resemblance between father and son was more pronounced than ever—watching them was like looking into reflected mirrors. But where Jahan was cold and haughty, Devendra looked pale and terrified.

"They're not," he said quietly. "And you can't let the Bookweaver destroy the Mages with her spell."

There was a pause, and the tension in the air made my stomach flutter.

"Come here, Devendra," said Jahan.

Devendra obeyed, his face etched with apprehension. His father seized his lapel, which glittered with military emblems. "How many medallions have you got?" he asked sharply.

His son gave a start before answering. "Seven, your Majesty."

"Seven," repeated Jahan. "Seven medallions from seven battles won by crushing seven disgusting rebellions."

He smiled terribly at the assembled lords. "Tell me, how does one win seven battles and remain such a coward?"

There was no answer, so Jahan turned on Devendra. "What do you think, *Commander*? Why are you such a coward?"

"Father," Devendra murmured. His eyes were closed, as though he was holding back tears—or rage.

"Answer me, son," the king hissed. "Why do you stand up for filth like the Mages?"

"*Father,*" Devendra muttered again, but it didn't sound like an apology.

It sounded like a warning.

"You imbecile," Jahan was saying. "You soft-bellied little boy. Answer the question!"

Even before Devendra opened his eyes, I knew what was about to happen. It was like everything he'd locked up for years had finally escaped him all at once.

"*I don't know!*" he shouted, and the marble at the base of Jahan's throne split, sending shards rocketing everywhere. I could feel the magic reverberating through the room, causing my blood to tingle.

And then the whispers started.

"*He's a Mage!*"

"*The king's own son.*"

"*Traitor.*"

Jahan's face was a mask, but Devendra's was pleading, expressive.

"Your Majesty," he began, and despite how much I hated him and all of the terrible things he had done, I felt a rush of pity towards him. "I didn't ever mean for this to happen. I just wanted to redeem myself—"

He flinched at the sight of his father's expression. It was beyond angry: it was disdainful.

"I knew you were going to be just like my brother," said Jahan coldly. "Pathetic, hopeless, never cut out to wield power. I sent you to hunt the Bookweaver because I hoped it would make a king out of you. But you remain, as always, a disgrace to the Zakir name."

"Your Majesty," Devendra tried again. For the first time, he looked nothing like the brutal military prodigy I'd always believed him to be. "Father—"

Somehow, I found my voice.

"Jahan," I said. "Leave Devendra alone. This is between you and me. *I* am the Bookweaver."

The king smiled indulgently, but there was no mirth in his face. "Look at that, son!" he said. "The Bookweaver herself has come to your rescue. Even she finds you hopeless!"

Devendra glared at me, but his eyes lacked their characteristic ferocity. "I don't want your help," he said.

His father chuckled. "Here I am, dedicating my reign to eradicating Mages, while one of them thrived within my own dynasty! I can't stand for that, can I?"

The king stopped laughing, his eyes steely against mine. "Which is why you and Devendra are going to fight to the death. Right here in my throne room."

I blinked, feeling as though I was free-falling.

Across from me, Devendra didn't look shocked or scared. He just looked angry. In one fluid motion, he had pulled his sword free from his belt.

The sound of scraping metal jerked me into action.

"Wait," I said. "Devendra, you don't have to do this. You don't have control over your powers yet, and I'm a fully trained Mage. If you fight me, you are going to lose."

His purple eyes narrowed. "Of course I have to do this," he said. "This is my only chance to live up to my father's legacy. Surely you'd understand that."

"No!" I insisted. "Your father clearly doesn't care about you. You don't have to prove anything to him! But together, you and I can do great things."

Devendra continued pacing, not taking his eyes off of mine. "I can do great things without you, Bookweaver."

King Jahan yawned. "Enough with the theatrics," he said. "You will fight now, or I will kill you both myself!"

I turned around, distracted, and that's when Devendra seized his chance.

Before I could react, his sword swung out of nowhere, lightning-fast. I staggered back, but my *sari* tripped me—Devendra's blade caught the shimmering fabric. I felt my feet leave the ground as I was thrown backwards by the sheer speed of the blow.

My elbows hit the ground with a painful jar—I looked up just in time to see Devendra coming in for another jab, and I rolled out of the way. The tip of his sword plunged deep into the marble floor.

In the moment it took for him to pull his blade free, I was back on my feet. I took a deep breath as his sword came slashing at me so fast it whistled. "*Temperus!*" I screamed, and a white-hot plume of fire erupted from me, arcing towards Devendra.

Somehow, Devendra managed to parry the flames, but the force of my spell knocked the breath out of him, sending him sailing.

For an instant, I thought I had him, but I'd forgotten that Devendra was still the imperial commander of Kasmira and a warrior to be reckoned with. He landed on his feet with catlike agility, charging with a fury I'd never seen in him before, because his father's honor—everything he'd ever valued—was at stake.

He lunged, and I dove out of the way. Before Devendra could change directions, I released a force field.

A wall of pure energy rolled across the floor, searing the marble in its wake. For a moment, all I could see was Devendra's face, shiny with perspiration and illuminated by magic. Then the force field hit him, and Devendra collapsed, his sword thrown from his hands.

My spell should have knocked him out, but Devendra seemed to defy all possibility as he staggered back to his feet. A cut above his eyebrow was bleeding freely, and his eyes were bugging with fury.

I took a step towards him.

"Devendra, we can stop," I begged. He glanced around wildly, but his sword was across the hall—he was defenseless. "We don't have to—"

Without warning, Devendra threw himself at me.

He was unarmed, but even so, he took me by surprise. For a horrible moment we struggled, and I could see the desperation in his eyes. Although he was swordless, he was still dangerously strong as he reached for my neck, fully prepared to kill me with his bare hands.

"*Ilumino!*" I gasped, and my magic cascaded through the air— Devendra landed hard on his back. An instant later, I was rushing towards him, fire whirling around me.

I saw him flinch as he raised his hands to protect himself, but bare flesh was no match for the magic of an infuriated Bookweaver. And for the third time, I thought I had him.

The next moments seemed to happen in slow motion.

A bolt of magic erupted from his hands, jet-black and thrumming, shredding my spell like a razor. Instinctively, I ducked, but Devendra's powers were so strong that I felt a wave of heat pass over me. Somewhere beneath the adrenaline, my heart rate slowed.

The crown prince had unlocked his magic.

A collective gasp spread through the court, but I wasn't listening. All I could feel was the afterglow of Devendra's spell.

He got to his feet, looking just as surprised as I was. But his initial shock passed quickly, replaced by a determined smile.

"Looks like I have a couple of tricks up my sleeve, Bookweaver," he said. As he spoke, he released another burst of white-hot fury.

I managed to repel him, but just barely. He kept blasting, pushing me back, foot by foot, until I was pressed against the wall. Time seemed to liquify as I stared into his eyes.

For a second, all I could see was myself, six months ago, cornered and scared, my magic seemingly with a life of its own. I hadn't been able to control myself then.

But neither could Devendra. I could take advantage of that.

Devendra reared back, preparing to blast me for a final time. His spell hurtled at me, and I took a deep breath. I raised my arms, closed my eyes, and reached for my magic, ebbing and flowing with my beating heart.

And in that moment, I created a Shield.

I felt the pain of his spell in my nerves, but only for a second, because the magic had rebounded upon its caster. Devendra looked horrified as he tried to retract the spell, but it catapulted towards him with an unconquerable fury.

Our eyes met briefly before he was slammed so hard that he skidded across the floor. His head collided with the base of Jahan's throne.

The crown prince seemed to shrink as I advanced, almost leisurely, coming in for the final blow.

I had the spell on the tip of my tongue, the magic in my blood. I was ready to strike him with the fire of a thousand suns—enough energy to avenge every person who had lost their life in Bharata.

But somehow, I couldn't move. I felt the magic tingling, but I was frozen in place, staring into his purple eyes.

I couldn't watch the life fade out of those eyes like it must have faded from my father's. Because I knew that if I killed Devendra, I'd never really escape the guilt. In the end, he still would have won.

"What are you waiting for?" snarled Jahan. "He's a disgrace. Put him out of his misery!"

Devendra was panting. "Do it," he said. "My father's right. Do it, please!"

"No," I said. "I'm not going to kill you. You and I are both worth more than that."

Devendra's eyes were shining with furious tears. "What are you doing?" he gasped. "You defeated me. This is the only way I get to die with any honor."

My stomach pulsed with mixed emotions—fury, pity.

"I don't care about your honor," I said. "This is about mine. We all have a choice, and mine is to never sink to your level. Because I'm the Bookweaver's daughter."

I glanced up at Jahan. "You're wrong. We're nothing alike."

The king appraised me coldly. "You've disappointed me, Bookweaver," he said quietly. "You're made of much weaker stuff than I imagined. Now, you will weave my spell, or I will kill the boy myself!"

I hesitated, and he sighed.

"It's not too late," Jahan said. "It's not too late to save them, you know."

As he spoke, the doors opened, and six people were dragged out by imperial soldiers: Naveen, Kira,

Nina, Niam, Aisha, and a brown-haired woman I didn't recognize. My blood felt cold beneath my skin.

For a moment, I thought about what it would be like if we died.

The thing is, it wasn't just the act of breathing that would cease—it was sunsets with Nina, the scent of flowing ink, rainy skies, spring *reya* blossoms, and laughter. These were the things that made leaving infinitely more painful.

I picked up the manuscript Sharati and I had written last night.

Naveen was shouting something at me, but I couldn't hear him. All I could hear were the words inside my head.

And I began to read aloud.

> *He was immortal. His glory threw the rays of the sun into despair. Entire empires fell to his iron-handed grasp as his army conquered, seemingly without end. All were at his mercy. King Jahan Zakir had the entire world at his feet.*

The sight of my friends, helpless and terrified, fueled the energy within me. Jahan, meanwhile, closed his eyes—I knew he could feel the magic, too.

> *Farkandh, Kampi, and Indira fell like crushed saplings, one by one. Blood lapped the king's feet—blood of the enemies—their final tributes to their rightful master. Piled by the thousands into dungeons, every man who whispered words against his king paid the price.*

And I continued, the Ancient Kasmiri as familiar as my breath itself, sliding off my tongue like I'd been speaking it for years. I could feel the magic expanding, reaching its crescendo, leaving me shivering with anticipation.

For the first time in my life, I was in the Yogi state.

Fear clung to hearts when the soldiers galloped through the streets. They were bloody, victorious soldiers, heaped with looted riches, showering it upon the kingdom. Upon the poor, who would rise up from the crevices of poverty; upon the children, who would rule the new nation in their wake.

It was like nothing I'd ever felt before. The words hit me in waves of unmatched magnitude, cresting and breaking. It was the same power I had felt the night I first unlocked my magic, but a thousand times stronger. For this time, I was every part of the raging whole. I was the master of my magic, in all of its unexpected beauty. I was my own infinity.

Then the king himself rode through, and their fear was assuaged.

I paused, and Lady Sharati handed me a quill to shape the runes that would change Kasmira's destiny. The court around me, hushed in anticipation, seemed to be a million miles away.

For the immortal man riding past was their ruler, Jahan Zakir, who would lead Kasmira into a golden age that the bards would sing about for eons to come.

"REYA!"

When his lips formed my name, the sound was almost involuntary.

It pierced through the chaos and hit me with staggering acuteness. Even from fifty feet away, even through the haze of magic, I knew it was Naveen. I turned around, searching wildly for the source of his voice. For a moment, our eyes met. My mouth called his name back, but faintly.

"Reya! You can't do this!"

Jahan leapt to his feet. "Make him shut up!" he screeched.

But Naveen, struggling and scratching, wouldn't stop. "You are the Bookweaver!" he shouted, panting. "Don't you understand? You are the only master of your power! You're the only one who can weave your destiny!"

His hand fumbled for something in his pocket. I stared in frozen awe as he tossed the book in slow motion. The war around him faded into senseless shapes. I couldn't feel the rush of the magic or the beat of my heart.

I could only see his eyes: his determined, polychromatic eyes.

The guards surrounding him leaped to grab the book, but it slipped between their fingers. Naveen collapsed, blood trickling from his brow. Suddenly, I knew what I had to do.

I seized *Ink Soul* out of the air, still warm with Naveen's heat. I opened the first page to see a forest of my own handwriting—except this time, my words weren't alone. Neatly inscribed beneath every page was Naveen's Ancient Kasmiri translation, familiar and powerful as my own breaths.

The problem with weaving stories is that you can never quite know when yours will begin.

And once your story has started, there is no turning back.

In the kingdom over blue waters, a dream vibrated through the land.

My voice was strong and clear, imbued with Ancient Kasmiri: the language of power and mystery of time immemorial. People lunged at me—guards, Sharati, Jahan alike—but I twisted aside, fighting them off with my free hand.

Jahan was still howling at me, but it all sounded muffled, as if from a dream. Maybe this was, indeed, just a dream.

It shone with the sun when it rose, and stayed gleaming in the people's hearts in the dark. It was a girl's dream that her kingdom would be free.

I used to wonder what death would feel like. If it was a sudden burst of flame, a spark, a single cry in muted lips. Or if it was a shadowy, steady heat, rattling and buzzing, a flurry of ash sifting into oblivion.

The girl was powerful, but she was terrified. Fear clung to her heart like mold, and the sun never warmed the darkest corners of her mind.

But now, as my voice rang through the hall, I knew what death felt like. It was a bright blaze, a surge of power, the creation of a legacy. It was about reaching high, even as you fell down. I finally understood the honor my father had sought to instill in me.

And so the girl set out on a journey. It was not a journey to flee the king whose evil knew no bounds, nor was it one to avenge the father she had lost. It was a quest to discover herself.

My name is Reya Kandhari. I am the Bookweaver's daughter. My legacy was always mine to weave.

She endured. She survived. She kept fighting for an abstract idea of freedom she had never known, yet strove to define. She put everything, including a city, on the line.
But then she lost.
The words that had danced through her spirit and soared through her soul died. She was gone. She was dead to the world.
There were small glimmers of hope. She found friendship and solace. A few words were revived.
Then it darkened once more. The girl knew she would succumb to the king. She swayed to his evil tunes— and she went to his side. It was dark. She was alone.

I was frantically writing to finish the story that I finally knew to be mine. My pen flew over the paper, the ink and parchment bonding together, shining and gleaming.

Then a candle flared up.

I saw them all with clear eyes. Nina, frightened but unconquerable as she tore free from her captor's grip. Naveen, his eyes blazing as he struggled against those who beat him with iron fists. The brown-haired woman's eyes, which were shining with pride.

> *The words returned—they ebbed and flowed, danced and soared about the girl, and she knew who she was: she was the Bookweaver's daughter, and she carried his legacy with pride. The pen flowed across the paper, weaving her legacy until all was still—the king was dead, and Kasmira was free.*

I dropped the quill. For a moment, all was indeed still. And then fire erupted from my core.

The *mahal* exploded, and the marble ceiling above me cracked with unstoppable power—huge shards of fresco fell sharp as rain, sending plumes of dust soaring back into the air.

I closed my eyes, willing the walls to cave in, forcing the sun to rise. The room erupted with light, a portrait of fiery ecstasy from the heavens themselves—

I was an avenging angel. I was Death herself.

Out of the corner of my eye, I saw a metallic streak—the Spider was soaring at me, silver arms alight with deadly magic. I stomped my foot and a fissure burst along the marble floor, but the Spider simply flew over it with inhuman agility. Its metal eyes were bright with fury as it reached for my throat—

It happened so fast.

I managed to dodge the object that whizzed over my head, but the Spider wasn't so quick.

I turned to see Nina, one arm still raised in mid-throw, as her shoe connected with the Spider's head, knocking its silver mask off with a satisfying *clunk*. We stared at the awful, pallid flesh underneath, something slimy and undead, as the Spider started to disintegrate. Just before it disappeared into smoke, the Spider's eyes met mine, and it formed three last words: *"It's not over—"*

Its words were cut short by a heart-stopping thud—the mighty oak doors had burst free, their hinges snapping under pressure.

I clutched *Ink Soul* to my heart, protecting it from the falling rubble. We had minutes, if not seconds, before the entire *mahal* came crashing down—

For a moment, everything seemed to slow down as the building caved in around us.

I watched in mingled awe and horror as the nearest column tumbled with a crash that sent dust billowing over the throne, and Jahan disappeared under the wreckage—

"NO!"

Devendra dove towards his father's body, even as sharp rocks rained down, narrowly missing him. I could see his terrified face, just like my own on the day my cottage burned down.

His lips parted in a scream, forming words: *"You killed my father!"*

"Devendra—"

He launched himself at me, and I felt the Spider's curse, which had lived within me for the past weeks, finally rip itself free from my skin.

Black flames coiled from my hands like whips, and I struck at Devendra. I could feel the Spider's curse transferring between us, piercing him, burning his face. I barely had time to register that *I was cursing someone* before he flailed backwards, right into the path of a collapsing staircase.

I closed my eyes, but it still didn't drown out the crash—

Then I heard her.

"Reya!"

It was my mother's voice.

I crawled desperately towards the sound, beyond caring whether or not it was a hallucination. All I knew was that I was clawing towards the light.

I made it to her arms just before I blacked out.

Twenty-One

"Mother?"

There was a violent rustling and a clatter of foot-steps.

"She's finally awake. Naveen, get over here quick!"

My eyelids felt a thousand pounds heavier, but I forced them open.

Nina, Kira, and Naveen were kneeling over me, their faces radiating concern. As the world came into focus, I realized I was lying on a burned mattress in the middle of a street.

Stabs of pain shot up my chest as Nina placed her weight on the mattress.

"How do you feel?" she asked, helping me up.

"I ache all over," I grunted, wincing as Nina lifted me into an upright position. "What just happened?"

I turned to see the hill in the distance behind me. Where the *mahal* once stood was a pile of smoking ruins—a shattered tower here, a collapsed wall there.

235

The remaining bricks on the hillside grinned like smashed-in teeth.

Naveen nodded grimly beside me. "You happened."

I turned around in alarm, and Nina took my hand to stabilize me. "It's been a week," she said. "You've been out for a whole week."

Everything came rushing back at once.

"Where is everyone? Jahan, Devendra, Sharati—"

Kira shook her head. "They're all gone," she said quietly. "Your *vayati* took out the entire *mahal*, sparing only the servants and the Renegades imprisoned inside. All the refugees set up camp in the streets outside the palace."

I took a deep breath, still struggling to process. "You're saying that I managed to destroy the palace and end nearly a decade of tyranny with one spell."

Nina took my hand. "You did it," she murmured. "You took back your magic, and you took back the kingdom. Things can only get better from here."

I turned to Naveen, who smiled at me. Bruises darkened his entire face, but he looked happier than I'd ever seen him. "Not bad, Bookweaver," he said.

I couldn't tear my eyes away from the sight of the palace. "Devendra?" I asked again. "You're sure he's dead—" I couldn't finish the sentence.

Nina nodded. "I'm sure. Your curse blasted him backwards, and he was crushed by the debris. There's no way he could have survived."

She couldn't quite hide the satisfaction from her voice. I knew I should share her glee that the prince who had tortured us was dead, but I couldn't help but feel a twinge of regret, because he had seemed more human than his father.

"What about the Spider?" Naveen was asking.

Nina shrugged. "He disappeared, or maybe he died, I don't know—"

I remembered the Spider's metallic hands reaching for my throat, and I couldn't help but shiver.

"You hit the phantom lord of death in the head with a shoe," I said wonderingly. Nina grinned, and I stared at her with a whole new awe.

"There's something else," Nina said, and this time she didn't even try to hide the emotion from her voice. "Someone escaped when you blew up the palace. Your mother, Lady Kamala. She's alive."

I spun around to face Nina. "My mother?" I started, but stopped mid-sentence—

I saw her. She was standing at the edge of the street, one hand on her hip, talking animatedly to Niam and Aisha. For a moment, I simply watched her. Then she turned and saw me.

I had forgotten her hair. I had forgotten her eyes. Years of pain and grief had blurred her features from my mind. But all of a sudden, they were back, and I saw her more clearly than I ever had in my life.

And then I was running towards her, all aches forgotten. She was saying something—I later realized it was my name.

"Mother!" I gasped, and we collided.

She was thin, wisp-like in my arms, and her brown hair was filled with more gray than I remembered. But she was still warm. And she still smelled like lily perfume.

Lady Kamala was crying when she released me. "I don't understand," I heard myself whisper. "I thought you had died—"

My voice broke off, a wonderful possibility occurring to me. If my mother had come back to life, then maybe, just maybe, Amar might be alive too …

But she was shaking her head. "No, Reya," she said quietly. "I never died. I've been here in the *mahal* all this time. You set me free."

The enormity of what she was saying hit me, and I felt my knees turn to water. "All this time?" I repeated slowly.

"All this time," she confirmed. And between her words, I felt the vastness of all we had lost, all of the milestones I'd piled up without her: seven years of memories, birthdays, jokes, conversations, and a thousand other things that a mother was supposed to share with her daughter, but we never did.

"But how did you survive?"

She sighed. "It's a long story," she said. "One, hopefully, that I have years to tell you."

Her voice sounded the same as I remembered, but not quite—there was a new note in it I couldn't identify.

"I pledged my loyalty to Jahan so that I could try to get on the inside. I tried to help the Renegades save your father's life. But I failed."

And now I recognized what was missing in her voice. When she spoke, her eyes mirrored my own grief. She'd been taken away from Kasmira for seven years and returned a widow. I suddenly realized that when I lost my father, she lost her husband.

"The note warning me about the Renegades' invasion—that was from you, wasn't it?" I asked.

Suddenly I was desperate for answers, desperate to fill in the missing years with my mother. She looked grateful for the change in subject.

"It was," she said. "After Bharata, Jahan decided he could no longer trust me. He was going to have me killed along with the Renegades. I knew that I had to save you."

Her eyes crinkled. "But you saved yourself. And I'm so proud of you, Reya."

There was so much to say, so much to ask. But Mother was right: we had years ahead of us to replace the ones we had lost. For now, I decided on the most pressing question.

I took a deep breath. "What do we do now?" I asked.

She smiled. "Now we heal," she said.

"I'll be here for you," I said. I took her hand, and together, we walked into the glorious sunshine.

Epilogue

It rained the day I finally said goodbye to my father.

The darkening sky unleashed its grief upon us, bleak and pure as winter. Gazing out at the icy deluge, it occurred to me that the rain pelting our cabin window might be the same rain that had once whistled against the mango tree, evaporated and repooled a thousand times over. It was almost as if we had come full circle.

Of course, so much had changed since that summer rainstorm. Three weeks had passed since I'd brought down the castle, and still there were problems to be solved: replacing Jahan, uniting Kasmira, bringing the lost Mages back home. But those could wait, at least until we had gotten our chance to grieve.

I heard a knock on the door, and my mother stepped into the cabin, shaking droplets from her long white shawl. There was something ethereal about the snowy flowers she had threaded through her graying hair. When she smiled at me, I understood for the first time why Kasmiris wear white to our funerals.

"Are you ready, Reya?"

"Of course, Mother," I said, offering her my hand. I was never going to get used to saying that.

She took my hand and together, we stepped out into the gloom, huddling together against the slanting rain. Her hand was slender but warm; only her wedding ring stamped an icy band against my skin.

The streets were empty except for the two of us. I watched our reflections in the continuous line of storefront windows, appearing and disappearing between panes of missing glass. We only vaguely resembled each other; I was the color of deep chai, petite against her pale, willowy frame.

Her eyes met mine briefly in the reflection.

"Reya, over here."

I turned and followed my mother's gaze. Without meaning to, I gasped.

I was looking at my childhood home.

It was as grand as I remembered it, despite its state of utter ruin. Half of the bungalow had crumbled; only the east wing stayed intact, and even its walls were sagging after seven years of neglect. But somehow, it was there. It had survived.

All these years I had lived in the *Raj*, and it had never occurred to me that our old home was still standing.

"Here?" was all I could say.

Mother nodded. "Home again," she said simply. "I think it's where your father would have liked to rest."

I followed her through the remains of the garden. The weeds were knee-deep; all of the little clay tigers and garden ornaments I remembered from childhood were gone, likely pillaged long ago. In the distance, I saw our fountain, cracked and overgrown with mildew. And above it, miraculously still aloft, hung the swing my father had once built for me.

The rest of the funeral party was already waiting by the garden stream, their heads bowed against the rain. They had all managed to find something white to wear. Looking at their faces, I felt an overwhelming rush of affection: Roshan, Niam, Aisha, Nina, Naveen, and Kira.

I took my place next to Nina as my mother began to speak.

"Thank you all for coming," she said. Her voice cracked, and I took her hand. She sighed. "It's just—I didn't expect to be saying goodbye to my husband like this."

There was a moment of quiet, and I realized that there were no ashes to scatter in the stream, as ancient Kasmiri tradition dictated. Jahan had even taken that from us.

My mother dabbed at the corner of her eye with regal composure.

"Amar and I built this home together," she said, indicating the ruins around us. "We thought we had years ahead of us to raise our daughter within its walls. And that's all he ever wanted: to raise the next Bookweaver into a woman of grace and compassion."

She smiled at me. "Even though he's not here, I know he got what he wanted. And—I just want to thank him for raising our daughter."

As she spoke, she slipped her wedding ring from her finger and placed it in the small stream, building a fleeting altar to my father. The ring sparkled as it was swept away by the current.

Roshan spoke up. "I'm going to say a few words

about my brother," he said. "Everyone else is gone—our parents, our siblings, our family. With Amar's passage, Reya and I are the last Kandharis, and I carry that name with pride."

He sighed, staring up into the sky. "It wasn't always easy to be the non-magical best friend of the Bookweaver. Sometimes it felt like I'd have to sacrifice everything for the sake of my brother's legacy."

Nina and I exchanged glances, and I quickly looked away.

"But that didn't matter, not in the end. Because Amar taught me that magical ability or inherited power are not what make a person great. It's their choice to keep trying, no matter how hard it seems, because giving up is simply unthinkable."

Next to him, Niam cleared his throat.

"Amar Kandhari taught me so much about bravery," he said quietly. "He showed my family kindness, and it's a debt I can never repay. All Aisha and I can do is try our best to help others. And somehow, that still isn't enough."

Aisha took his hand, and he held onto his sister for support. For a fleeting moment, I wondered what it would be like to have a sister of my own: another brown-haired, dark-skinned, green-eyed girl to give me strength in the hardest moments.

Then I realized that I didn't have to wonder. I had Nina.

"Thank you, Niam," Mother said. "Reya?"

She was looking at me, but I couldn't find the words. My throat had closed up.

"Goodbye, Father," was all I could choke out, reaching behind my neck for the last time. I unfastened the cracked pearl that had once been the center of my existence, letting it drop into the stream with a splash.

The sun was beginning to shine as our party dispersed. Only Naveen stayed back.

Nina and my mother looked back as they left, but I shook my head, indicating that they should go on without me.

Naveen and I walked through the ruined garden in comfortable silence. He, too, was wearing white—a buttoned white top that had somehow survived the *mahal's* explosion. His hair, still ruffled from the rain, glinted copper in the weak sunlight, giving the impression that his head was on fire.

"Thank you," I said at last. Naveen looked sideways at me. His pace was leisurely enough, hands jammed into his pockets with a practiced casualness, but I could tell that he was upset. I suddenly remembered that he, too, had lost his parents at a young age.

"Coming here was my pleasure," he said. His hand brushed my arm reassuringly, and my heart warmed— I hadn't realized how badly I needed his human presence, to be touched, to be heard.

"No. I meant ... thank you for everything." Our eyes met, and I tried to put so many unspoken things into one sentence: *Thank you for fighting for me. For listening to me. For believing in me, even when I didn't believe in myself.*

He understood, and I saw the side of his mouth curl up in his characteristic half-smile.

"You would've done the same," he said. He turned, and I followed his gaze to see a lone plant, its silver flowers bright amidst the tangle of weeds. Naveen knelt down and picked up a single blossom.

"I don't know what it is, or how it survived," he said, tucking it behind my ear, "but it's beautiful."

"I know," I said. "This was my father's favorite flower. The crown of *reya*."

About the Author

Malavika Kannan is an 18-year-old writer from Orlando, Florida. While *The Bookweaver's Daughter* is her first novel, Malavika's writing has appeared in *Harper's Bazaar*, *Teen Vogue*, the *Washington Post*, *HuffPost*, *NYLON*, and *VICE*, and she was named a National YoungArts Winner, two-time Scholastic Art & Writing medalist, and Library of Congress writing winner. A relentless advocate for female empowerment, Malavika founded the Homegirl Project to help girls discover their magic and change their communities.

You can keep up with her at malavikakannan.com.